This book must be returned by the date specified at the time of issue as the DATE DUE FOR RETURN.
The loan may be extended (personally, by post, telephone or online) for a further period if the book is not required by another reader, by quoting the above number / author / title.

Enquiries: 01709 336774

www.rotherham.gov.uk/libraries

All she had to do was give him back the ring.

THE DOCTOR'S RUNAWAY FIANCÉE

BY
CINDY KIRK

First Published in Great Britain 2016
By Mills & Boon, an imprint of HarperCollins*Publishers*
1 London Bridge Street, London, SE1 9GF

© 2016 Cynthia Rutledge

ISBN: 978-0-263-92012-3

23-0816

Our policy is to use papers that are natural, renewable and recyclable products and made from wood grown in sustainable forests. The logging and manufacturing processes conform to the legal environmental regulations of the country of origin.

Printed and bound in Spain
by CPI, Barcelona

From the time she was a little girl, **Cindy Kirk** thought everyone made up different endings to books, movies and television shows. Instead of counting sheep at night, she made up stories. She's now had over forty novels published. She enjoys writing emotionally satisfying stories with a little faith and humour tossed in. She encourages readers to connect with her on Facebook and Twitter, @cindykirkauthor, and via her website, www.cindykirk.com.

To Patience Bloom, my wonderful editor,
whose presence in my life has made it so much richer.

Chapter One

Sylvie Thorne gazed into the beauty-shop mirror and forced herself to breathe. Seven seconds in, then out for eleven. Almost immediately, the panic ebbed.

Two hours earlier she'd given Cassidy Duggan, owner of the Clippety Do Dah Salon, free rein to cut and color her hair. While Cassidy was as nontraditional with hair as Sylvie was in cake designs, there was no better stylist in Jackson Hole.

"What do you think?" Cassidy fussed with a stray strand of hair and smiled expectantly.

"I look…different." An understatement to be sure, but the best Sylvie could muster.

As she continued to study the unfamiliar reflection, Sylvie reminded herself she was the one who'd asked for a change. She'd grown bored with the hairstyle she'd had since high school. The upcoming wedding of a friend had been the gentle shove she'd needed to try something different.

Two hours ago she'd walked in with wavy copper-colored hair hanging in loose curls halfway down her back and put herself in Cassidy's experienced hands.

"Sleek and sophisticated." Daffodil Prentiss, the hairstylist from the next booth, punctuated her proclamation with an approving nod.

Sleek and sophisticated.

While those two words were rarely tossed in her direction, Sylvie cocked her head and opened her mind. "I like it."

The waves had been straightened and the blunt cut hair now barely reached her shoulders. The muted copper strands, while still the predominant color, had been replaced at the ends by several inches of soft honey blond.

"Are you sure?" Cassidy asked, apparently troubled by her less-than-enthusiastic response. "If you don't like it, I can—"

"Exactly what I wanted." Sylvie spoke more decisively this time. "And the change I was looking for."

"I didn't want to go too crazy." Cassidy tapped a finger against her bright red lips. "If you get home and decide this isn't enough of a change, we could try some cerulean blue. I think the color would make those violet eyes of yours really pop."

"No blue needed." Sylvie spoke quickly. "This is perfect."

Because of the nontraditional bakery products produced in her Mad Batter kitchen and the boho-chic styles she preferred to wear, Sylvie was aware many saw her as "quirky."

Now, at least according to Daffodil, she looked sleek and sophisticated. Who'd have thought that was even possible?

"Stellar job," Sylvie assured Cassidy. She rose from the salon chair and gave the stylist a hug.

While Cassidy ran her credit card, Sylvie chatted with Daffodil. After adding a generous tip, she stepped out into the bright summer day and let the sunshine warm her face.

She ran her fingers through her hair, gave her head a toss, feeling suddenly light and carefree. It was as if she'd shed the weight of the past along with her hair.

As early September was still too early for skiers to begin their descent on Jackson Hole, the downtown foot traffic was relatively light. Sylvie found herself glancing down the walkway, looking for someone she knew, eager to show off her new do.

Hair and friends were quickly forgotten when her gaze settled on a dark-haired man at the end of the block. She studied his profile as he read the menu posted in the window of the Coffee Pot Café.

Sylvie's breath froze. She brought a hand to her throat. *Andrew.*

Her heart slammed against her rib cage, then began to thud heavily. A roaring filled her ears. She told herself it couldn't be him. Andrew O'Shea lived in Boston, two thousand miles away. Yet something about this man was all too familiar.

In their months together she'd often told Andrew that he wore wealth and privilege like most men wore a favorite coat. He'd laugh as if she'd made a joke.

While it was true he came from money and never had to do without, as a physician he'd been passionate about improving the lives of others. Working as a concierge doctor allowed him to practice medicine while still having time to dabble in the family business.

As she stared unblinking at the man, a wave of yearning washed over her. The sensation was so strong it brought tears to her eyes.

"Sylvie?"

Stifling a groan, she blinked back the tears before turning.

Josie Campbell, her closest friend and bride-to-be, touched Sylvie's arm. "Is something wrong? You had the strangest expression on your face."

Sylvie glanced down the street and discovered Andrew's doppelgänger had vanished. She offered an easy smile. "For a second I thought I saw someone I knew."

Josie followed the direction of her gaze. She was a pretty woman with honey-blond hair, clear green eyes and a diamond the size of Grand Teton on her left hand. "What does she look like?"

"He." Sylvie waved a dismissive hand. "Tall with dark hair. I'm sure it wasn't him."

"Tall and dark, huh?" Josie brought a finger to her lips. "Would it be accurate to add *handsome* to that description?"

Andrew was indeed handsome. But he was in Massachusetts, not strolling the streets of Jackson.

"*Handsome* would be accurate. If we're talking about your fiancé." As a tall, broad-shouldered man headed straight for them, Sylvie's words slid into a smile.

With Josie's back to her fiancé, she didn't see his approach.

"Noah is very handsome." Josie's lips curved. "I'm supposed to meet him at the church. We're—"

Dr. Noah Anson stopped his future wife's words by spinning her around. When her mouth opened in a surprised shriek, he kissed her soundly.

Josie's arms wrapped around his neck and he gently stroked her back as the kiss ended. The look of love in Noah's eyes took Sylvie's breath away.

The yearning she'd experienced moments earlier returned with the force of a tsunami.

Expelling a happy sigh, Josie slanted a teasing glance at her future husband. "Before we were so rudely interrupted, I was saying Noah and I have an appointment with Pastor Johnson at the church. With the wedding less than a month away, there's still a few loose ends we need to tie up."

Noah kept an arm around Josie's waist, gave Sylvie a nod. Then he inclined his head, two lines forming between his dark brows. His gaze narrowed. "There's something different about you today."

"It's the hair." Josie smiled her approval. "With all our talk about hot guys, I forgot to say how much I love, love, love the cut. And the color is simply fabulous. Cassidy, I presume?"

Sylvie fingered one of the short silky strands. "Who else?"

The Clippety Do Dah Salon might have a cutesy name, but Cassidy Duggan produced sophisticated results.

"Looks good on you." Noah paused, the words Josie had uttered moments earlier appearing to finally register. "What hot guys?"

"Why, you, of course, darling." Josie rose on tiptoes to brush a light kiss across his lips. "And some guy Sylvie spotted that she knew."

"On first glance he looked familiar," Sylvie clarified. She waved a dismissive hand. "It wasn't him."

It couldn't be Andrew. There was no reason for him to be here.

Still, an uneasy feeling settled over her shoulders and Sylvie found herself scanning for the once-familiar face all the way to her shop.

Later that day, Dr. Andrew O'Shea wandered into Hill of Beans in downtown Jackson and ordered a coffee. He took the cup of the Ethiopian blend to a table by the window.

It felt strange to be dressed in blue jeans and a polo on a weekday. Back in Boston, Andrew rarely wore jeans. But as he packed for his trip to the land of cowboys and rodeos, he'd tossed in a pair.

The last thing he wanted was to stand out. His plan was to remain inconspicuous until he figured out how best to approach Sylvie.

Andrew had thought about simply popping into her shop. He'd already scouted out her location, so that remained an option. But interrupting her during a business day didn't feel right, and he was a big believer in going with his gut.

Still, he wouldn't wait much longer. He'd flown in yesterday. This morning he'd eaten at a local café, the Coffee Pot, and planned his strategy. He was past ready to put to bed the tangled emotions he'd carried with him the last few months. Once he got the answers he sought, he'd return to Boston and move on with his life.

When Sylvie had run off shortly before their wedding, he was stunned. He'd called around, but no one seemed to know where she was, but neither were they surprised. Apparently Sylvie had a reputation for being capricious.

Andrew had decided to give her a few days to come back on her own. Before twenty-four hours had passed, his legs were knocked out from under him a second time. He learned a close childhood friend was dying. All the pain of Sylvie's leaving had been pushed aside while he dealt with a more immediate crisis.

Shortly after his friend passed away, he'd read an article about the Jackson Hole Wine Auction and Food Festival. A local cake artist, Sylvie Thorne, had been featured.

Andrew had discovered she'd relocated to Jackson Hole. He just hadn't realized how much seeing her smiling face in that magazine would affect him. His world, which had been off its axis since Sylvie's leaving, had tipped even further. It still hadn't fully righted itself.

Even if Sylvie's name hadn't been mentioned, Andrew liked to think he'd have recognized her work in the full color photograph of the multilayered wedding cake with the fondant skull. Even when they'd been together and she was still developing as a cake artist, she'd had a recognizable style.

He recalled the cake she'd made for his birthday shortly before she left. It had been a three-layer castle— a Spamalot version—with crooked turrets and gargoyles with big toothy grins.

Cradling the mug in his hands, Andrew stared out the window. He now sat only blocks from the place where she created her masterpieces.

He had to admit he wasn't sure how it was going to feel to finally be face-to-face with his runaway fiancée.

Andrew lifted the strong brew to his lips and took a long sip. One thing was certain—he'd come for answers.

He wasn't leaving Wyoming without them.

Sylvie eased the ancient minivan to the curb a block down from Benedict and Poppy Campbell's home in Spring Gulch. Instead of hopping out, she remained in the vehicle and tried to recall just why she'd accepted an invitation to the backyard barbecue.

She rarely attended dinner parties or barbecues as a guest. But then, she didn't meet friends at the Coffee Pot Café after church on Sundays, either. Heck, she didn't even go to book club, though reading was a favorite pastime.

Part of the reason for her reticence had to do with not growing up in a world where people had dinner parties or barbecues. She hadn't known book clubs even existed. As a child, she hadn't known anyone who read for pleasure.

Sylvie and her mom had been too busy trying to survive to think about books. Subsisting on groceries bought with food stamps, their "home" had been a run-down apartment courtesy of public housing.

When her mother took off and left her when she was thirteen, Sylvie had discovered that life was even worse in foster care.

She pushed the painful memories aside and reminded herself those times were over and done. When she'd moved to Wyoming, she promised herself no looking back. She'd stuck to her vow.

With the exception of earlier in the week, when she thought she'd seen Andrew on the streets of Jackson. That night, she'd pulled out her engagement ring and done some reminiscing.

Though her heart still ached whenever she thought of him, Sylvie still believed that leaving Andrew had been the right decision.

Keeping his ring, however, had been wrong.

It didn't matter that the three-carat diamond had been her last connection to him.

It didn't matter that the ring wasn't a family heirloom.

It didn't matter that she had a good reason at the time for taking the piece of jewelry with her. She'd feared Andrew might be so distraught over her leaving him that he might fling the ring, one that had been specially designed for her, off the Longfellow Bridge and into the Charles.

Sylvie closed her eyes briefly. The trip down memory lane had dumped her spirits into the basement. Would it really be so horrible to drive off? No one had seen her. There was still time for a quick getaway.

The only reason she hesitated was that this party was for Josie. Her friend had made it clear she wanted her maid of honor to attend.

Giving in to the inevitable, Sylvie opened the van door. She stepped out, careful not to brush up against the dusty side of "Ethel," the 1996 Dodge Caravan she'd purchased shortly after arriving in Jackson Hole.

Though some of the light blue paint had peeled and there was a dent in the back from a shopping cart gone wild, the van started like a dream. Once she'd had the seating in the back removed, it had a good-sized cargo area for hauling cakes.

As Sylvie gazed over all the shiny vehicles lining the street in this affluent Jackson Hole subdivision, it struck her that Ethel didn't fit in here any more than she did.

Sylvie glanced down at her skirt with its orange, red and black diagonal stripes and hesitated. For tonight's festivities she'd coupled the skirt with gladiator sandals and a black tank. Skin showed from a few inches above her belly-button ring to just below her navel.

This barbecue would bring together the movers and shakers of Jackson Hole. She'd be as out of place here as she'd have been in Andrew's world.

Coming tonight had been a mistake.

Sylvie was reaching for the door handle when Tim and Cassidy Duggan pulled behind her van in a shiny red SUV, boxing her in. She heaved a resigned sigh, then walked over to greet Cassidy and her husband.

Marriage and motherhood hadn't changed Cassidy. The hairstylist wore a bright blue skirt with an animal-print tank. The bold pairing eased Sylvie's trepidation about her own outfit.

Though Cassidy was married to a prominent pediatrician, from what Sylvie knew of the woman's background, it mirrored her own humble beginnings.

After an exuberant greeting, Cassidy looped her arm through Sylvie's on the walk to the house, asking if she'd brought a cake to the barbecue.

"No cake, but I whipped up a batch of cupcake burgers." Even though Poppy, the hostess, had insisted she didn't need to bring anything, Sylvie had dropped off the novelty treats earlier in the afternoon.

She'd told Poppy it was so she didn't have to bring them with her tonight. The truth was, delivering the promised treats early had left the door open to skipping the party.

Cassidy's husband, Tim, dressed conservatively in khakis and a navy polo, cocked his head. "Cupcake burgers? Sounds like something Esther and Ellyn would enjoy."

Esther and Ellyn were Tim's twin girls from his first marriage. A widower, Tim had raised the girls alone until he and Cassidy had married last year.

"I bet they'd love 'em. They sound so unique and fun." Cassidy tapped a finger against her lips. "Are cupcake burgers difficult to make?"

"Super easy. You start with vanilla cupcakes and a tray of brownies." As they covered the short distance to the porch, Sylvie explained how she cut circles of brownies for the burger and used colored frosting for the mustard, ketchup and lettuce wedged between the vanilla cupcake "bun."

"You're amazingly talented." The sincerity in Cassidy's voice had warmth flooding Sylvie's heart, even before the stylist added, "Not to mention you look absolutely stunning tonight."

The simple compliment was the confidence booster Sylvie needed as Poppy opened the door. Despite being seven months pregnant with baby number two, the hostess looked elegant in gray linen. She greeted them warmly, giving each of them a quick hug.

Sylvie lost Cassidy and Tim on her way to the back patio. She'd expected to see a grill or two, maybe several picnic tables and a few lawn chairs. Instead an outdoor barbecue "kitchen" embellished with stone accents was the focal point of the large patio. Tea lights hung on brightly colored ribbons from thick branches of leafy trees that provided an umbrella of green.

A pergola extended over an outdoor kitchen bar, where the buffet had been set up. Bouquets of brightly colored flowers sat amid a multitude of decorative bowls filled with a variety of salads. Sylvie spotted her cupcakes with the other desserts. The nearly empty baking-sheet-turned-decorative-fabric-tray told her the cupcakes were a hit.

Benedict and his father, John, manned the grill, which filled the air with the delicious scent of roasting meat. Poppy seemed to be the official greeter while her mother-in-law, Dori, was making sure everyone had a drink and mingled. Unlike parties where hired help did the serving, this barbecue appeared to be a family effort.

Sylvie accepted something called a Crazy Coyote Margarita from Dori, then caught sight of the bride-to-be across the yard chatting animatedly with several women. Josie saw her at the same moment and motioned her over. The excited smile on her friend's face told Sylvie that coming to the party this evening had been the right decision.

With a spring in her step, Sylvie stepped off the flagstone patio and onto the lush green grass. She had paused to take a sip of her drink when the back of her neck began to prickle.

An instant later, a hand closed around her arm and a familiar masculine scent washed over her.

"Hello, Sylvie."

She turned and stared into the brilliant gray eyes of Andrew O'Shea.

Chapter Two

From the second Sylvie walked through Ben Campbell's front door, Andrew didn't take his eyes off her. Running into Ben, a friend from prep-school days, had been fortuitous. Other than Sylvie, he hadn't expected to see anyone he knew in Jackson Hole.

The invitation to a barbecue was appreciated, as was Ben's warm handshake. Yet Andrew had been fully prepared to offer an excuse until Sylvie's name was mentioned. Ben had been telling some story about his sister, and Andrew had been stunned when his former fiancée's name popped up.

Congratulating himself on keeping his cool, Andrew had asked if that was the baker who'd recently been featured in an article on Jackson Hole's Wine Auction.

At Ben's assurance that they were speaking of the same person, Andrew steered the conversation back to the barbecue and learned Sylvie would be there. He'd accepted the invitation on the spot.

Now she was standing in front of him, looking as beautiful as ever. Her hair was different, not as curly and now with blond tips, but it was her.

While he'd had the advantage of knowing their paths would cross this evening, the look of shock in her eyes mirrored what he was feeling. It made him glad that, at least for the moment, they were alone.

A polite mask settled over her elfin features, and her eyes now gave nothing away. "Andrew. What a surprise. I didn't expect to see you here."

"Ben and I went to school together." Hating that he felt as gauche and unsure as a sixteen-year-old, Andrew shoved his hands into his pockets and willed his heart rate to slow.

It didn't help that she had on the same perfume she'd worn when they were together: a slightly citrusy scent that made him think of orange groves and lovemaking. His pillow had retained the scent for days after she left him.

The hurt that had taken root in his heart since he got her text—a damn *text*—telling him the engagement was off and she was leaving was still there. But right now that hurt was mixed with an unholy anger that seared his veins.

"I best go back inside." She spun around and might have escaped through the door, if his reflexes hadn't been so good.

His hand shot out, closing around her bare arm like a vise. "Don't walk away. Not again."

Displaying surprising strength, Sylvie jerked her arm back.

Andrew had been poised for battle until he saw tears pooling in those large violet eyes. Resisting a nearly overwhelming urge to wrap his arms around her, he stepped back and held up his hands.

If she bolted, he wouldn't stop her. That didn't mean he wouldn't get his answers; it just wouldn't be this evening. He could wait.

"I agree we need to talk." She brushed back a strand of hair from her face with a hand that trembled slightly. "But this isn't the time or place. This is a celebration of Noah and Josie's engagement. I don't want anything to spoil the evening for them."

Andrew couldn't help thinking of the last party he and Sylvie had attended. It had been held at his parents' home in Boston. Though not a formal engagement party, it had been a family celebration to introduce her to Andrew's extended family. It had been elegant and tasteful, and Sylvie had hated every minute of the gathering. Andrew suddenly recalled that she'd offered to make a cake for the event, but his mother had demurred that it would offend the caterer.

Both he and Sylvie had known the real reason. His mother was worried about the kind of cake Sylvie would make. He'd let Sylvie down that night, Andrew realized. At the time, it hadn't seemed a big thing.

But this wasn't about recriminations and who had dealt the other the biggest slight; this was about achieving closure. "I'm available later."

The second the words left his lips, he realized it had been a lame thing to say. And when her lips quirked in a slight smile, Andrew realized something else. Her smile still carried quite a punch.

"Tomorrow?" she asked.

He nodded. "Lunch."

It struck him just how blasted civilized they were being.

She gave a nod.

He pulled out his phone. "Give me your number."

Sylvie glanced back toward the house and shifted from one foot to the other. "I'll call you." She paused. "Unless you've changed your number."

"No change." His eyes met hers. "You changed yours."

Sylvie lifted one thin shoulder but offered no excuse. When he cocked his head expectantly, she recited her new number while he keyed it in and then read it back to her.

While the tightness around her eyes revealed her stress, when she spoke, her voice was casual and offhand. "Appears you and I are reconnected."

They'd been very connected once until she'd abruptly severed the tie he'd been convinced would last forever. She'd done it with a single text. A handful of typed words that said she didn't love him, couldn't marry him and didn't want to see him again.

Yes, they'd once been connected. Not anymore.

Sylvie wrapped her mouth around a juicy hamburger with avocado relish and peppered bacon and wondered if she could possibly be dreaming. She'd had vivid dreams in the past, all involving Andrew.

Not a single dream had concerned food or a barbecue. Most slipped in during the night hours and were of a sexual nature.

In those dreams, she felt Andrew's smooth lips against her mouth, her throat and her breast, and his touch heated her body to a boiling point. When she awakened, usually right before full consummation, she was filled with an ache that brought tears to her eyes.

The ache was never simply physical. *That* Sylvie could easily have handled. The intense longing for the man she'd loved—that was not so easily put aside. Those vivid dreams would drag her down and wreak havoc on her emotions for several days until she became strong enough to put her focus back on the here and now.

If she'd learned one thing from thirteen years with an addict mother and subsequent years in foster care, it was that sometimes just getting through each day was a victory.

"Your friend is really hot." Josie sidled up beside Sylvie and slipped her arm through hers. She took a sip of her margarita and slanted a sideways glance. "Why is it you never told me about him?"

Seeing the speculative gleam in her friend's eyes, Sylvie dropped the burger to her plate and waved away the question with a careless hand. "The only hot man we should be discussing tonight is your fiancé."

A softness filled Josie's eyes as her gaze strayed to linger on the lean dark-haired man currently speaking with Josie's father. She gave a little laugh. "Did you ever imagine me with a neurosurgeon?"

"I recall you saying once that I should slap you silly if you ever so much as gave any doctor a second glance." That conversation had taken place shortly after she and Josie became friends. "Then all of a sudden you're dating Noah. Now you're going to marry the guy."

"What can I say? The heart wants what it wants." Josie's tone waxed philosophical. "I can't imagine my life without him, Syl. I just overlook that he's a doctor."

Sylvie chuckled, even as an ache filled her heart. When she was with Andrew, she'd done her best to ignore that her boyfriend was not only a doctor but a zillionaire heir to O'Shea Sports.

She'd been fooling herself, thinking a mutt from the wrong side of the tracks could be a good match with a Boston purebred.

"What's the matter?" Josie's hand settled on Sylvie's shoulder, the touch as gentle as her voice. "Tell me."

Almost immediately, Sylvie lifted her lips in a well-practiced smile. "I'm thinking of everything I need to get done this week. I have a last-minute party for the Sweet Adelines I snagged when their previous caterer poofed. An upsurge in business is a good thing, but when you're a one-woman show, it can feel a bit overwhelming."

"If there is anything I can do to help…" Josie's eyes were dark with concern.

"It'll be fine." Or it would, Sylvie thought, once Andrew O'Shea went back to Boston. Back to his world, back where he belonged.

After a restless night, Sylvie rose early and immediately pulled out her phone. She stared down at it. She didn't want to call Andrew. She'd moved on. Why dredge up the past? If she opened that door, she feared all the feelings she'd worked so hard to submerge these past months would rush to the surface.

Still, she couldn't dis him. She couldn't be that cold. Not to someone she loved—er, had once loved.

Even if fairness and compassion weren't issues, there was the matter of the ring. It didn't belong to her. When

Andrew had proposed, she accepted the diamond as a symbol of the pledge they'd made.

Today, they would make their peace. She would return the diamond and close the door on that piece of her past.

The truth was, she'd felt like a coward running off in the middle of the night. Fleeing under cover of darkness was too reminiscent of what her father had done when she was four, and what her mother had done nine years later. Except with them there had been no note or texts.

They'd simply disappeared from her life and she'd never heard from either of them again. When she'd left Boston, she told herself what she was doing was different, that it was for Andrew's own good. She still believed her leaving was best for him.

But thinking it over now made her wonder if that was what her father, and her mother, had believed.

After placing the call, Sylvie spent the remainder of the morning deciding what to wear. Five clothing changes later, she pushed open the door of the Coffee Pot Café. Her fingers clenched and unclenched as she glanced around the crowded restaurant. She spotted Andrew at a small table by the window.

The moment he saw her, he pushed back his chair and stood.

Always the gentleman, she thought with a bitterness that made no sense.

After lifting a hand in acknowledgment, she zigzagged between the tables to him. Though Sylvie had met many people in the months she'd been in Jackson Hole, she was grateful none of them were in the main dining room. The last thing she felt like doing was making small talk.

As she drew close Sylvie realized that, as always, Andrew looked perfectly put together. While he might have left his suit and tie back in the hotel room, he still managed to look elegant in dark pants and a gray button-down cotton shirt, open at the collar.

Suddenly conscious of the casualness of her simple peasant skirt and ribboned lace top, Sylvie lifted her chin and reminded herself this was Jackson Hole, not Boston. They were having lunch at the Coffee Pot, not one of his private clubs.

He pulled out her chair as she drew close. "You look lovely."

Sylvie took a seat and glanced around. A baby wearing a pink crocheted hat several tables over met her gaze and began to cry.

Andrew didn't appear to notice the wails. His entire focus remained on her.

"I may have miscalculated."

He resumed his seat, his brow furrowed slightly. "How so?"

"I didn't realize the place would be so busy." Or that the seating was so tight. The table next to them was scarcely two feet away. Though Sylvie didn't recognize the couple sitting there, that didn't mean they didn't know *her*. "Hardly conducive…"

She let her voice trail off, not surprised when he nodded. With Andrew she'd never had to complete thoughts. From the moment he walked into the Back Bay Bakery, where she'd been working after graduating from a New York City culinary school, they'd been on the same wavelength.

They kept the conversation centered on the weather until the waitress had taken their order. Sylvie ordered a salad, though she wasn't sure she'd be able to eat. Not with the way her stomach pitched.

Once the waitress left, Andrew's gaze returned to her and she felt the impact of those gray eyes all the way to her toes. "That was an impressive article on you related to Jackson Hole's Wine Auction."

Sylvie traced her finger around the water glass, absently wiping away the condensation. "Is that how you located me?"

"I knew where you were within a week of you leaving Boston."

Startled, she dropped her hand and looked up. "You knew where I was, yet you didn't come after me?"

Andrew lifted his own glass of water and took a long drink. "You made it very clear in your *text*—"

The jaw muscle jumped again as Andrew paused. He appeared to carefully consider his next words.

"You said you didn't want to see me again." He spoke slowly and distinctly in a low tone, the words for her ears only. "You made it clear what we had was over."

"I'm sorry about the text." The fact that she'd texted him her goodbye seemed to be a particular bone of contention. She had to admit if he'd done that to her, she'd have been furious. More than that, she'd have been crushed. "I really am sorry. I thought if you wanted more of an explanation, you'd follow me. But you didn't."

Sylvie wasn't sure what had gotten into her. She'd been happy, *relieved*, he hadn't come after her.

"Audrey collapsed the morning after the party. I

was at the hospital when I received your text." Andrew paused as the waitress dropped off their drinks.

Two tables down, the baby began to wail in earnest.

Andrew glanced down at the coffee he didn't want and felt the rage he'd kept contained for the past three months threaten his tightly held control. That day had been the worst of his life. It was as if the world around him had imploded.

He couldn't believe the woman he loved, the woman he'd planned to *marry*, had, for no discernible reason, decided she didn't love him anymore and walked out. Still reeling from that shock, he'd learned a close friend from childhood was terminally ill with cancer. He hadn't even known Audrey was sick.

The baby's piercing cry broke through his thoughts. He rubbed the bridge of his nose where a headache was trying to form. Coming here *had* been a bad idea. A busy café on a Sunday morning was no place for a serious discussion.

He shouldn't have come to Jackson. Hadn't Sylvie made it clear by her words and actions that she didn't want him? Andrew O'Shea didn't run after any woman, even one he loved. *Had* loved, he corrected.

He would leave. Thank her politely for her time and walk out the door. Why did the reason she'd left him even matter? The fact was, she'd walked out on him. That couldn't be undone.

Andrew took a deep breath. "Tha—"

Her hand closed over his. They weren't soft, do-no-work hands, but ones with strong fingers and clean, blunt-cut nails. A hand with just a hint of calluses on the palm. A hand that smelled faintly of citrus.

"I'm sorry about Audrey." Sylvie's voice grew thick with emotion. "She was a wonderful woman."

The words took him by surprise. "You knew Audrey had cancer? That she passed away?"

Sorrow filled those violet eyes. "Just recently I read the piece on her in the *Globe*. It was quite a tribute."

Audrey had been a talented musician, Juilliard-trained, and came from a prominent Boston family. The piece, tastefully done after her passing, had been not only a testament to all the lives she and her family had touched in their philanthropic endeavors, but also a tribute to a beautiful young woman who died way too young.

"She and I were friends for as long as I can remember." Andrew found himself thinking back. Quite unexpectedly, his lips quirked up. "When we were thirteen, or perhaps it was fourteen, we made a pact that if we weren't married by the time we were thirty, we'd take that trip down the aisle together."

Andrew had turned thirty at the beginning of the year, right around the time he'd met Sylvie.

"You didn't marry her."

It was such an odd thing for her to say that for a second Andrew wondered if he'd imagined the words. "Audrey was like a sister to me. There was never anything more between us than friendship."

Sylvie glanced at her untouched cup of coffee. The baby had grown silent, too.

"Andrew, I—"

"Tell me about your life here," he said brusquely.

Those thickly lashed violet eyes widened. "Wh-what?"

Impatiently he gestured with his head to the couple

beside them. The man and woman, both in their thirties, had quit talking to concentrate on their food. Or to listen?

Understanding filled her gaze. As if she needed to gather her thoughts to answer his simple question, she took a long sip of tea before responding.

"Even back in culinary school, I knew I wanted to open my own business." Her eyes took on a faraway look. "My craft is important to me. It's a passion. I'm an artist, not simply a baker."

Andrew shifted uncomfortably in his seat. He'd known she loved to bake, er, create. Heck, she'd been working in a bakery when he met her. He'd known she enjoyed making cakes. But had he realized it was her passion? Had he cared?

Something in knowing she'd found it so easy to embrace a new life—one without him—to explore that passion stung. "Starting a business takes capital."

She flinched at his tone and Andrew cursed the defensive response. And the coldness that chilled the words.

But when she responded, it was with a slight smile. "You haven't seen my shop. If you had, you'd know that a business can be launched on very little capital. My goal was to secure an inexpensive space that could be brought up to meet all necessary codes. I succeeded."

Should he tell her that he had seen her place, or rather the outside of the business she called "the Mad Batter"? It looked like a hole-in-the-wall, with only a door and a sign. Not even a window.

He decided that might show too much interest. "Is your shop near here?"

"Not far." Sylvie paused as the waitress brought the food and set the plates on the table.

He watched her lower her gaze to the salad, then slant a glance at his omelet and side of bacon. Despite the stress of the past few minutes, he found himself smiling. "Go ahead."

She picked up her fork, stabbed a piece of romaine. "I don't have any idea what you mean."

He lifted a piece of bacon and waved it in front of her. "You know you want it."

For a second Sylvie hesitated. In the next, she'd snatched it from his fingers and taken a bite. As she munched on the piece, a rueful smile tipped her lips. "I'd given up bacon. I was trying to be good."

"I led you into temptation."

She opened her mouth, then shut it. "Some things are irresistible."

Was she remembering that time long ago—it felt like a lifetime—when she'd told him *he* was irresistible?

This time when the baby began to cry again, Andrew barely noticed. He was too focused on the woman sitting across the table from him. He'd forgotten how lovely she was, with that coppery brown hair, those big violet eyes and that heart-shaped face. No wonder he'd fallen in love with her.

Ever since she'd left, Andrew tried to figure out why he was finding it so difficult to move on. He must have asked himself a thousand times what had attracted him to Sylvie. Sitting across from her at this tiny table at a café that boasted plastic flowers in copper coffeepots for centerpieces, he understood.

She was different than any of the women he knew,

and that had intrigued him. Not to mention, not a single female of his acquaintance possessed Sylvie's beauty and unique style.

She walked out on you. There's nothing special about that.

Andrew lifted an eyebrow. "Do cakes pay the bills?"

After popping the last bite of bacon into her mouth, she took a moment to chew and swallow. "Pretty much. I do them for weddings and other special events. I've recently begun providing baked goods to various places in Jackson Hole. The chef at the Spring Gulch Country Club and I are in negotiations for services. I get by."

"A far cry from the Back Bay."

"That was your world."

"It could have been yours."

"No." She sat back in her chair and met his gaze. "You're wrong. It would never have been mine."

Chapter Three

Sylvie shoved a piece of arugula into her mouth and decided meeting Andrew at the Coffee Pot had been a mistake. Not only was it too public for any serious discussion, but she didn't want to have a serious discussion about anything with Andrew. What would be the point?

It wasn't *his* fault that they came from two different worlds. She'd been foolish to fleetingly believe love would be enough. But love hadn't kept her parents together. Love hadn't even made her mother stick with her child, even though she'd been the only family Sylvie had left.

Andrew might have thought he loved her, might even have convinced himself he did, but it had been only infatuation. An infatuation that could have cost him everything that mattered in his life.

When she'd overheard him and his father heatedly arguing—about her—she knew she would not be the cause of a rift between Andrew and his parents.

The only purpose of meeting with him again was to give back a ring she was no longer entitled to keep. A clear break with the past would allow her to move on in a way she hadn't been able to do in June. Dropping her fork to the table, she slid her hand inside her fringed bag.

Before she had a chance to pull out the diamond, Andrew leaned forward. His fingers closed around her arm.

"No need to pay yet. We haven't finished eating. Besides, this is my treat."

The baby's sudden cry was like an ice pick in her eye.

Sylvie clutched the ring tightly in her palm. She'd loved the filigreed set and emerald-cut diamond from the second he'd placed it on her finger. Though it made no sense, Sylvie wanted to keep the ring.

She couldn't force a smile and this time she didn't even bother to try. "It was a mistake."

She wasn't sure what "it" she meant. Not exactly.

"You're getting real good at running. Better be careful or it might become a habit."

She met Andrew's gray eyes and released the ring back into the inside pocket of her bag. "I simply don't see the purpose to this."

"You owe me an explanation." Before Andrew could say more, someone called out her name. Then his.

Sylvie turned to see Ben and Poppy Campbell making their way to the table.

"What are you two doing?" Poppy asked.

"Uh, eating," Sylvie said, though she couldn't have downed another bite of salad if her life depended on it.

Poppy's laugh was low and husky, as perfect as her simple red sheath and boxy jacket. Here was a woman who would have fit perfectly into Andrew's world. Classy with a capital *C*.

When Josie had told her Poppy was a social worker, Sylvie was disbelieving. Fashion model? Absolutely. Social worker? No way.

Sylvie could easily believe that Benedict, in his dark brown pants, ivory shirt and Italian loafers, had been Andrew's schoolmate. Right now Ben's shrewd gray eyes were as curious as his wife's.

Apparently deciding the best response was a strong offense, Andrew smiled. "Sylvie and I were acquainted when she lived in Boston. We thought it'd be nice to renew our…friendship."

Blast him for that tiny hesitation that gave an extra punch to the last word. The implication that there had once been more between them was there. That was obvious when her two friends exchanged knowing glances.

Ben looked amused but not particularly surprised. "How fortunate, then, that I ran into you and invited you to the barbecue."

"I'd planned on looking up Sylvie anyway." Andrew spoke smoothly. "But it was a surprise to learn we had a common friend."

Sylvie wasn't sure Dr. Benedict Campbell, one of Jackson Hole's leading orthopedic surgeons, considered her a friend, but she wasn't about to protest.

"A bunch of us meet here each week when the kids are in Sunday school. We have a large table toward the back." Poppy stepped back to let the waitress slip around her to top off Andrew's coffee cup.

Sylvie saw Andrew's gaze follow the gesture to an alcove at the very back of the dining area where a large rectangular table sat, three-quarters full.

"We've asked Sylvie to join us many times," Poppy said pointedly. "She always turns us down. At least now we're in the building at the same time, so I'd say we're making progress."

Sylvie smiled. She liked this social worker. The ones she'd dealt with growing up had always seemed more concerned with their rules and regulations. Poppy seemed to genuinely care about everyone.

"Join us?" Poppy pressed.

"We appreciate the offer," Andrew said, before Sylvie could politely refuse *again*, "but we've got a lot of catching up to do."

We? Sylvie's head began to spin. Had he really said *we*? As if they were together beyond this lunch. And why was his hand closing over hers, giving it a proprietary squeeze?

No. No. No.

When she attempted to pull her hand back, those strong fingers merely tightened around hers. His hand remained in place until Ben and Poppy said their goodbyes and wandered off to join their friends.

Once their backs were turned, Sylvie jerked hard and finally freed her hand. "What was that about?"

Instead of answering, Andrew calmly lifted the napkin from his lap and placed it on the table. She noticed he'd barely touched his food. "I'm finished eating. How about you?"

"I'm done." She stared down at the salad, and a rush

of emotion swamped her. While she'd cried buckets of tears after leaving Boston, seeing Andrew reminded her how dear he'd once been to her...and how easily she could once again become attached to him.

She would return the ring. There would be no reason then for her to see him again.

"Andrew." She swallowed hard. "I kept your ring. That was wrong. I apologize."

For a second he looked confused, as though he'd forgotten about the three-carat flawless diamond. When he finally did react, he waved the words away as if the ring was of no consequence. "I gave it to you. It's yours."

"You gave it to me when we made a promise to each other," Sylvie insisted. "But—"

"I don't care about the damn ring." Abruptly, Andrew pushed back his chair with a clatter and stood, tossing several bills on the table. "I do care why you ran out on me. We'll discuss that at your place."

People seated around them stared with a curiosity that had Sylvie scrambling to her feet. While she would never live her life according to others' expectations, she was a business owner—a new business owner—in Jackson Hole and preferred not to encourage idle gossip.

Sylvie forced a smile and an easy tone. "Sounds like a plan."

On their way out of the café, she tolerated the palm he placed against the small of her back. But once they were outside and standing in front of a closed insurance agent's office, she whirled.

"What kind of game are you playing? What do you want from me?"

He raked a hand through his hair, blew out a breath, but didn't immediately answer.

"I'll give you back the ring. Then this will be done." She flipped open the flap of her purse, but once again he stopped her.

"Not here." He took her arm and began striding down the sidewalk, his jaw set in a hard line. "At your shop."

Had he always been this dictatorial? She pulled her eyebrows together and struggled to match his long strides. Andrew had always been decisive, no doubt about that. But she saw an arrogance here that she didn't much care for.

Of course, what did it matter? In short order he'd be out of her life, this time for good.

He stopped abruptly, steadying her when she stumbled. "On second thought, this might be better done at your home. Where do you live?"

Sylvie blinked, her head spinning as if she was seated on an out-of-control Tilt-A-Whirl.

"Your home address." Impatience sounded in his suddenly gruff voice. "What is it?"

Her heart began to beat wildly. Something in his tone, in the set of his jaw, brought memories from her childhood flooding back. She wanted to run, but her feet wouldn't cooperate.

As if he sensed her distress, his eyes softened. "This is more difficult than I want it to be."

His deep voice was suddenly as smooth and placid as Lake Jenny on a summer day.

"I live in the back of my shop." Sylvie began to stride with purposeful steps in the direction of her business.

The sooner she gave him the ring and answered his questions, the sooner he would go.

Andrew caught up with her but made no move to touch her. Instead he simply fell into step beside her. "Do you like living and working in the same location?"

"It has its advantages."

They walked in silence for another minute.

"The cost of housing in Jackson Hole is sky-high," she said when the silence continued. "I didn't realize that when I moved here."

"How'd you pick here?" His tone was conversational, as if he, too, was determined to avoid the uncomfortable silence.

"I'd been here before." She lifted a shoulder in a slight shrug. "I remembered it as a magical, beautiful place."

There was the barest flicker in his eyes. Sylvie might have missed it if she hadn't been looking right at him. He'd made the connection. Remembered that she'd come here with him. They'd taken the trip on a whim, shortly after they started dating. He taught her to ski and how to throw a proper snowball.

It was during that trip to Wyoming that she'd fallen in love with Jackson Hole and with him.

Silence descended again. This time neither of them made the effort to break it.

He stepped to the side when she reached the cobalt blue door of the Mad Batter and pulled out her key. Sylvie still wasn't certain why she'd brought him here, why she hadn't simply insisted they conclude their business on the street.

You owe him.

"Spartan digs."

She turned at the sound of the voice and realized that Andrew had stepped inside what she referred to as "the order room." Not much larger than a deck of cards, it contained a small round table and two chairs.

"What happens if you have more than one visitor?" Even as he spoke she saw his gaze checking out the gleaming vinyl floor in a black-and-white checkerboard pattern and the cherry-red cushions on the chairs. Bright spots of color in an otherwise unimpressive area.

"Someone has to stand." Sylvie flashed a quick smile. "Plus, it seems to motivate the customer to decide quickly on what they want."

"Where are the ovens?"

It appeared Andrew expected a tour. Well, that wouldn't take long. Not when the entire space she rented was smaller than his walk-in closet.

She stepped inside the kitchen, unable to stop the flush of pride at the sight of the commercial ovens and stainless countertops. Even the air smelled clean. And it was all hers. Hers and the First National Bank of Jackson's.

"Impressive." He sounded as if he really meant it. "You mentioned you live here, too. Where's your apartment?"

"*Apartment* is much too glamorous a term for where I live." Sylvie gave a little laugh as he followed her through yet another door.

Inside the postage-stamp-sized room sat a twin bed—sans headboard—pushed against a wall. The only other furniture was a microwave on a stand and a straight-backed chair that had clearly seen better days.

She swept a hand to encompass the small area. "Home, sweet home."

Though he was obviously trying to hide his shock, he wasn't pulling it off.

Andrew cleared his throat. "This is…all of it?"

"No, there's more."

The tight stiffness in his shoulders eased. He smiled. "I knew this couldn't be all."

"There's a three-quarter bath through there." She gestured with her head through yet another door. "So you see, it isn't quite as small as it appears."

Confusion blanketed his face. He cocked his head and stared. "Why do you live like this?"

"The rent in Jackson Hole is crazy." He wanted honesty? She'd give him honesty. "Besides, small has its advantages. This spot is warm and dry and…cozy."

And beats sleeping in the van, she added silently.

His lips quirked up in a reluctant smile. "You always did have an optimistic nature."

Sylvie blinked. She couldn't recall anyone ever telling her that before. Was it true? Or was it just one more thing Andrew had seen in her that simply wasn't there?

She suddenly was conscious of just how tiny a space surrounded them and that she and Andrew were alone in this *cozy* space.

So close that she inhaled the scent of him. The cologne he wore was subtle and expensive. From day one, the enticing fragrance had the power to make her insides quiver. But how he smelled was only a very small part of what had drawn her to him.

The way he looked would have captured any single woman's interest. She loved the way his hair glimmered, looking as soft as mink's fur in the fluorescent lighting. She remembered how it had felt to slide her fingers through the thick strands. Maybe because he always looked so impeccable, she'd made it a point to mess up the stylish cut when they made love.

Naked, in bed, with his hair all tousled and a hint of a five o'clock shadow, he hadn't looked like a doctor or the heir to the third-largest sporting-goods company in the United States.

During those glorious times, it had felt as if they were on equal footing. It had been easy to forget all the ways they were different.

Too easy.

"Sylvie."

His voice was low and husky, filled with an emotion that brought a warmth to the single word.

She looked up and realized Andrew was right. There. Less than a foot separated them. He stood so close she could see the dark perimeter that surrounded the smooth gray of those gorgeous eyes framed with long, thick lashes. So close the scent of his cologne teased her nostrils, transporting her back to a time when they were happy and everything seemed possible.

"I told myself I wouldn't do this," he muttered.

Her heart was pounding so hard Sylvie felt light-headed. She inclined her head in the merest of movements. "Do what?"

The words sounded breathy, which was exactly how she felt at that moment…breathless.

"This." He jerked her to him and covered her mouth with his.

When Andrew thought of his best attributes, *well disciplined* came immediately to mind. He'd been a sensible child and had grown up to be a sensible adult. In the important matters of his life, he prided himself on carefully weighing the pros and cons of various options before making a decision.

Then he'd met Sylvie Thorne, and *sensible* no longer seemed to be a word in his vocabulary.

He pulled her up against the length of his body as he ravished her mouth. It was as if he'd been in a desert the past three months and had finally found water.

Warning flags popped up one after the other in his head, but Andrew paid no heed. The need rushing through his body was too strong to deny.

He'd intended for the kiss to be brief. Unfinished business tied up nice and tight. But once his mouth had found hers, Andrew forgot how to think. He reveled in the familiar feel of her slender body with the small breasts pressed against him. When that full, sweet mouth opened to his probing tongue, Andrew breathed a prayer of thanks.

It was as if ninety-five days had melted away and all he knew, all he wanted to know, was in his arms. Everything seemed right in his world now.

When her hands stole around his neck and her fingers slipped into his hair, desire exploded like fireworks over the Charles River.

Her moan, a low sound of want and need, only further fueled the fire burning in his blood. Andrew continued to kiss her, sweet, gentle kisses at first, then long, passionate ones that soon had his heart hammering against his chest wall.

The taste of her was so familiar that he forgot all that separated them and let himself simply go with the moment. He slipped his hand under her shirt and stroked the smooth warm skin of her back. They continued to kiss until he felt drugged with emotion.

Easing his hands up her sides, he stopped just under her breasts. When she wiggled slightly in frustration, he cupped the small mounds and then teased the nipples to hard peaks with his thumbs.

Her head fell back. As she moaned with pleasure, satisfaction rippled through him.

Lifting her loose-fitting shirt, he leaned over and covered the tip of one breast with his mouth.

She inhaled sharply when he began to suckle, her fingers tightening in his hair. "Yes, Andrew. Oh, yes."

It was all the encouragement he needed. Minutes later they tumbled onto the bed, their clothes scattered across the floor. Though the warning flags continued to pop up, Andrew barely noticed.

Drunk on the taste, the smell, the feel of her, he wasn't sure he could have stopped even if a stop sign had bopped him in the face. He certainly didn't want to stop. As he thrust inside her, her body closed around him like a tight glove. It took everything to hold back.

Andrew wanted this to last. For her. For him.

He slowed the pace, scattering kisses down her neck, murmuring sweet words as he did so, licking the sensitive area behind her ear and watching her respond with a mew of delight.

Before long, it felt as if they were racing headlong to the finish line at Suffolk Downs with a clear track ahead. Her hips pistoned, keeping pace with his thrusts.

When she cried out and went over the edge, Andrew dived headfirst after her, not wanting to let go of her, not wanting the connection to end.

Chapter Four

Sylvie had never had an out-of-body experience. But as she lay on the bed with Andrew's warm, naked body pressed against hers, she wondered if she was having one. For the first time in months she was at peace. If this was what an out-of-body experience felt like, bring it on. For now she would relish the comfort it brought to her.

Gently she glided her hand down his silky hair, then stroked his neck. Sylvie had always loved his body with the broad shoulders and tight abs, the lean hips and muscular legs. The slight patch of chest hair now tickling her breasts was familiar and comforting.

She'd missed him. She'd missed this closeness. She could admit that now. What was the harm? After all, this wasn't really happening, so she could indulge without guilt. He was her personal two-pound box of chocolates.

She planted a kiss against his neck and sighed. There had been only one man before Andrew, a boy in high school. That mistake had steered her away from intimate relationships for many years. Until Andrew had strode into the bakery where she'd been working.

Sylvie remembered that day as if it had just happened. The second she saw him, the air that had smelled of cinnamon and yeasty goodness had begun to sizzle. She'd been so taken aback by the unexpected sensations flooding her body that she'd barely spoken. He came back the next day and the next. After a week they'd been conversing easily and indulging in some flirting.

When he asked her out to dinner, she'd said yes. It had been the beginning of a free fall she'd been powerless to stop.

If she'd only known then what she knew now, would she have had sex with him that night?

She started to sigh and then realized she couldn't quite draw a deep breath.

"I'm crushing you." The deep voice sounded near her ear, and suddenly the pressure against her body was gone, along with the comforting warmth.

Sylvie's blood turned ice-cold. She blinked once. Blinked again. Those piercing gray eyes remained focused on her face.

With a hand that trembled slightly, she reached out and touched his bare shoulder. Only then was she forced to accept he wasn't an apparition but a flesh-and-blood man.

I slept with Andrew.

Desperately needing to put some distance between them, she placed both hands against his chest and gave a hard push. To her amazement he tumbled off the bed and landed on the floor with a loud thud.

She'd forgotten the size of the bed and hadn't considered that the only place for him to go was off the side. Lifting herself up on one elbow, Sylvie leaned over.

A wry smile lifted Andrew's lips as he pushed himself up to a sitting position. "If you'd wanted me off the bed, you could have just asked."

"You are really here."

He smiled. "As opposed to…?"

Warmth flooded her face. "This." She gestured with one hand between her and him. "It felt like a dream."

A look she couldn't quite decipher—and wasn't convinced she wanted to figure out—crossed his face. Before saying another word, he rose to his feet and began pulling on his clothes.

She took the opportunity to do the same.

"The sex was always good between us." He tossed out the comment and finished buttoning his shirt.

She tugged on her shoes. No point denying the obvious. "It was."

As if wanting to relax the suddenly tense atmosphere, Andrew took a seat on the rickety chair and gazed unsmiling at her. "Tell me why you left."

Though he hadn't come right out and said "tell me why you left *me*," the accusation hung in the air between them.

Feeling already a little weak in the knees, Sylvie plopped down on the edge of the bed and turned to face him. "I sent you a text—"

"We were engaged to be married and you sent me a text." Despite his calm demeanor, ice-cold fury underscored the words.

Sylvie resisted the almost overpowering urge to wring her hands. And her second impulse, which was to flee.

You're getting real good at running, he'd told her. The words—and her fear they might prove true—had her staying put.

"Leaving that way was my only choice." She lifted her chin, met his steely-eyed look with an unflinching one of her own. "I was concerned if we spoke face-to-face you might change my mind."

"Were you?"

Sylvie shivered at the coldness in his tone, at the hot anger in his eyes. She couldn't recall ever seeing him like this before. The Andrew O'Shea she knew was always so affable. An easygoing guy with a warm smile.

He wasn't smiling now.

"Don't you think, after all we shared, you owed me more than a *text*?" He spit the last word as if the taste was bitter as anise on his tongue.

"I wasn't the woman you thought I was," she said. "You fell in love with someone who didn't—doesn't—exist."

The fact that he'd been willing to sever relationships in his family for her sent a chill down Sylvie's spine.

"You're right about one thing." Andrew leaned forward. He rested his forearms on his thighs, his gaze never leaving her face. "I don't know you. The woman I thought I knew would never have walked away from me without an explanation."

Anger resonated strongly in his voice, but it was the hint of hurt she heard that had shame coursing through her veins like milk gone sour.

"You owe me an explanation." Abruptly he sat back. "I'm not leaving without one."

This was good, Sylvie reassured herself even as panic threatened. It was best they clear the air, so they could both move on. The trouble was, how much to tell?

As if he sensed her hesitation, his gaze sharpened. "The truth, Sylvie."

Her laugh, intended to sound casual, reverberated with nerves instead. "Do you want me to put my hand on a Bible and raise my right hand?"

"Don't be flippant."

Sylvie didn't feel flippant, just incredibly weary. And sad. Sad that their once bright and shiny relationship had become tarnished with guilt and recriminations.

She straightened her shoulders and drew in a steadying breath. Hadn't she always told herself she couldn't go wrong telling the truth? But if she told him about the conversation she'd overheard, he might be angry with his father.

No, she didn't have to tell Andrew the whole truth, just enough so her leaving would make sense.

"You were like no man I'd ever known."

"You haven't known all that many."

Sylvie flushed, realizing they were talking apples and oranges. "I wasn't referring to intimately."

Andrew already knew she'd been a neophyte in the sexual arena when she met him. One time with a seventeen-year-old boy didn't make a girl an accomplished lover. In fact, when Andrew and she made love, it had felt like her first time.

"I was referring to the kind of men I'd grown up around." Her lips curved in a slight smile as she remembered the first time she'd seen him. "You dazzled me."

He didn't return the smile, only continued to stare intently at her face.

She licked her lips. The words that she'd hoped would smoothly flow seemed to have hit a logjam. "I—I'd never known anyone like you."

"You say that as if it's a bad thing."

"I'd worked hard to get through high school and then through the culinary institute. I'd always been proud of my success. But when I was around you… I felt…less."

Andrew had admired her work, but she knew he'd thought it was just a hobby. That misconception wasn't his fault. She'd kept just how much it mattered from him. Looking back, she wasn't sure why she'd never told him that her art—her baking—was what had sustained her during all the lonely years she'd been on her own.

His gaze sharpened. "You think I didn't appreciate all you'd achieved?"

"Not you." Dumping this into his lap would serve no purpose. "Forget it."

"My family?" he pressed.

She thought of his mother and father. Though they'd been less than thrilled about their son becoming engaged to a woman outside their social circle—and putting that ring on her finger within months of meeting her—they'd been cordial. Besides, she firmly believed nobody could make you feel inferior without your permission.

"It wasn't anything anyone did or said." She placed her open palm against her heart. "It was me. This is such a cliché, but I felt like a square peg about to be pounded into a round hole."

She wasn't sure what she expected him to say. Perhaps nod and say he understood? Or maybe agree that indeed they were so different it amazed him their relationship had lasted as long as it had?

Instead Andrew steepled his fingers beneath his chin and gazed at her like a scientist must study a bug under a microscope. "You never said a word about those feelings, at least not to me."

The censure in the calmly spoken words stung like a hard slap.

"Being around your family and friends that night made me realize that you belonged with someone more like, well, like Audrey." Sylvie closed her eyes for a second, struggling against the grief welling up inside her. Though she hadn't known Audrey Cabot long, she'd liked her and considered her a friend.

"I never thought of Audrey in that way. She was a friend, nothing more."

It wasn't only her grief simmering just below the surface. The pain in Andrew's eyes told her just how much Audrey's recent death from cancer had impacted him.

"You can't honestly believe there was anything between us," he added.

"No, I know there wasn't." Sylvie had believed him when he'd denied any romantic interest in Audrey, but that didn't mean she didn't think they would have made a great couple. "I just mentioned her because Audrey always seemed more—"

She paused, searching for the right word.

He arched an eyebrow. "My *type*?"

"Exactly." She nodded, pleased he was finally getting the gist of what she was saying. "While I admit that you and I have amazing chemistry when it comes to sex, I think some of our decisions to get so close so fast was based on that chemistry. It wasn't as if you really knew me."

But really, whose fault was that? She was the one who'd held back, who hadn't let him get to know her fully.

Andrew's eyebrows pulled together in a puzzled frown. He rubbed his chin and his expression changed from puzzled to thoughtful.

"I couldn't imagine the woman I loved leaving me like that…and then sending me a text." His laugh didn't contain even an ounce of humor. "I didn't even rate a Dear John letter."

The knowledge that she'd hurt him stung. Bringing Andrew pain had never been her intention. She loved him. She wanted only the best for him.

Unfortunately, it had become apparent—to everyone but him—that *she* wasn't what was best for him.

"I'm glad I came to Jackson Hole and we had this talk."

Sylvie nodded.

"I'm also glad that we had sex."

She cocked her head.

"It reminded me just how powerful the chemistry is between us." His lips lifted in a slight smile for only a second. Then he was all serious again. "Undoubtedly the stellar sex made us think there was more between us than actually existed."

Sylvie stopped a frown desperately trying to form and reminded herself this realization was what she had wanted. She wanted him to see their engagement had been a mistake. Then why did she have to fight the sudden urge to argue with him, to insist that it had been about more than sex?

"S-sounds logical," she stammered.

"This should be simple." He muttered a curse, pushed to his feet and began to pace.

Sylvie uncurled the leg she'd tucked beneath her and rose so she was standing. Though he was still a good five inches taller than her, being upright made her feel as if they were on equal footing. "It appears we're ready to close the door."

Pasting a polite smile on her face, she waited for him to agree. Then she'd give him the ring, he'd say his goodbyes and leave.

Instead he stared, his gaze searching her face.

"It might feel that way to you." Andrew spoke slowly and deliberately, a frown still furrowing his brow. "The problem is, I find myself still wanting you."

Her heart, she was ashamed to admit, gave an excited little leap before she slapped it down. Not knowing how to respond, Sylvie remained silent.

"I believe more drastic measures are needed." He took a step closer, lifted her hand and brought it to his mouth.

Her heart skipped several beats then began to thud. "What k-kind of measures do you have in mind?"

"Immersion therapy."

Sylvie gave a strangled laugh. "Isn't that when you go to a foreign country and don't know the language?"

"In this case, I will immerse myself in your life." His unsmiling gaze met hers. "I obviously didn't know you before, Sylvie. What better way to get you out of my system than to become acquainted with the real you?"

Chapter Five

Allow Andrew to immerse himself in *her* life? The thought terrified Sylvie. The months since she'd left Boston had been difficult ones. There had been days when she'd been sorely tempted to pull the covers over her head and simply remain in bed.

Though walking away from him had been the hardest thing she'd ever done, Sylvie believed her decision to leave had been the right one. A life with the wrong person never ended well. She only had to look to her parents' marriage to validate that point. According to her mother, her relationship with Sylvie's dad had turned rocky shortly after they'd married. She'd never been able to make her husband happy, because they were just too different.

Given time, Sylvie believed it would have been like that with her and Andrew. Despite the explosive chemistry between them, he'd have come to his senses one day and realized they were simply too different. Unfortunately, by that time his relationship with his own parents might have been damaged beyond repair.

We might have been happy.

It was her heart whispering the words, not her head. Her head recalled the conversation she'd overheard between him and his father. Recalled the harsh words spoken between father and son.

From the shadows Sylvie had found herself silently siding with his father. Agreeing with him that she and Andrew *were* an unlikely pair. Nodding silently at his pronouncements that it *would* be a miracle if their marriage lasted more than a year or two. Like Franklin O'Shea, Sylvie believed that if she hadn't shown up Andrew would have fallen in love with someone of his own…well, kind.

When Andrew had insisted his father accept Sylvie or else, Sylvie realized she couldn't—she *wouldn't*—come between Andrew and his father.

Sylvie sensed Andrew's gaze on her face, still waiting for her reaction.

He was good at waiting.

She'd discovered that early on when he'd come into the bakery for eight days straight.

He'd been patient then. She sensed he'd be patient now.

"Okay." She lifted her shoulders in a slight shrug. "A couple of days—"

"As long as it takes."

As she caught the determined glint in his eyes, she felt the need to clarify. "Not forever."

He gave a soft chuckle. "I have to be back in Boston by October 1. No, not forever. I blocked out three weeks. I doubt it will take that long."

Three weeks with Andrew. She considered. "What would I need to do?"

"Be yourself."

That sounded simple enough. Three weeks. Twenty-one days of her life. Given their history, it seemed little enough to ask.

The fact that they'd hopped into bed almost immediately made her wonder if he was expecting sex to be part of the deal. "I think it is best we keep any physical intimacy to a minimum."

His gaze never wavered, though for a second she swore his lips twitched. "If that's the way you want it to be."

"I think it'd be best, don't you?"

The second the question left her lips, Sylvie wished she could smother it under a stack of pillows. Why was she asking for buy-in? This was her decision.

"If you're asking if I think it'd be a good idea for us to spend the next three weeks in bed." He paused and tapped a finger against his lips. "However much fun that might be, I'd say no. But I am open to considering anything up to that point."

Sylvie's voice deserted her. Her quickening pulse was completely illogical. The level of sexual interaction wasn't a big issue, she told herself, because sex was a nonissue. It took two to tango and she wasn't doing any more dancing with Andrew.

"I'll have work to do while you're here." She stepped into the kitchen. Normally she found comfort in the spotlessly clean room that already held so many pleasant memories.

But right now, Sylvie felt as if she'd just chased a Red Bull with a Java Monster.

Andrew had followed her into the room and she crossed the room to put some space between them.

Resting his back against the counter, he surveyed her with hooded eyes. "I'll help you pack."

Her eyebrows slammed together. "What are you talking about?"

"I'm staying at a friend's home in Spring Gulch. He only uses it during ski season. You'll stay with me."

Not asked, she noted. Told. She crossed her arms across her chest. "Not necessary and unworkable."

He raised an eyebrow.

"Not necessary because we can spend time together during the day." Sylvie blew out a breath. "Unworkable, because, well, just because it is."

He smiled. "If you recall, we didn't live together in Boston."

There were good reasons for that. Sylvie had been living with a friend in an efficiency unit not far from the bakery. He'd been staying at his parents' home until renovations were completed on his high-priced condo in Millennium Towers.

Though Andrew had invited her to stay with him at his parents' home—and his suite of rooms was certainly large enough for two—she hadn't been able to bring herself to agree.

"Perhaps if we *had* spent more time together, we wouldn't find ourselves in this position now," he mused.

"Hard to know for certain," Sylvie said equitably. "But I can't live in Spring Gulch. It's too far out."

"You can tell me why you feel that way outside." Without waiting for agreement, he opened the exterior door and held it open. "It's too nice a day to spend cooped up in here."

"You're not getting your way on this point," she muttered, brushing past him.

The sidewalks around her shop teemed with tourists. Women in capris and men in cargo shorts wandered in and out of the shops.

Andrew began to walk. "Let's check out the Town Square."

"It'll be even busier there," she warned, even as she fell into step beside him.

Up ahead four antler arches stood at the corners of the George Washington Memorial Park, commonly referred to as the Town Square.

Sylvie heard herself babbling about the arches, instead of articulating all the reasons she couldn't move in with him. "The Antler Arches are a huge tourist draw. Did you know each arch is made up of two thousand antlers? Many of the elk antlers were harvested by the Boy Scouts after winter sheds."

If he found it odd she was such a wealth of information about a community she'd only recently begun to call her own, it didn't show. As they covered the last block, she added a little more history about the arches gleaned from a trip to the Jackson Hole Historical Society one rainy afternoon.

Sylvie had been surprised by how quickly this place— so far from where she'd grown up—had begun to feel like home. Perhaps it was because the people here seemed to appreciate individuals who forged their own path. Or maybe it was because Jackson Hole residents embraced the arts. Sylvie had been amazed by the number of painters, sculptors and writers who made their home here.

Jackson Hole was also an athletic community where residents skied, biked and jogged as much as the weather would allow. Even Sylvie, who'd never considered herself particularly athletic, had recently begun hiking the trails and doing a little cycling.

Yes, Jackson Hole was her home now, in ways Boston had never been, never could be.

Sylvie cast a questioning glance in Andrew's direction. "Want me to take a picture of you under the arch? You could send it to your family."

He didn't even crack a smile at her teasing tone. "Tell me what you have against Spring Gulch."

She expelled a heavy breath.

"I don't have anything against the area." The subdivision outside the town of Jackson was one of the nicest in the Hole. "It's lovely. I'm sure your friend's home is lovely."

She still found it hard to swallow that someone would purchase a home in such a pricey area and not live in it year-round.

A muscle in Andrew's jaw jumped. "You agreed to spend time with me."

"I start baking at three a.m.," she told him. "I don't want to drive all that way in the middle of the night. Right now all I have to do is roll out of bed, open the door and I'm there."

As they strolled through the crowds, Sylvie could almost see his mind considering, weighing her words, considering his response.

It was just too bad he hadn't used the same restraint before jumping into a relationship with her.

"I see your point."

Relief surged. "This immersion thing doesn't have

to include being in the same house while sleeping. In fact, my not being there at night might be for the best."

"I agree that having you drive into Jackson alone in the middle of the night isn't smart."

In the process of rejoicing over the small victory, Sylvie nearly missed his next comment.

"I'll drive you."

Startled for a moment, Sylvie could only stare. "That's too much to ask."

"I don't agree."

They strolled back down Broadway in the direction of her shop.

"That was the issue back in Boston." His voice was firm, resolute. "We didn't spend enough quality time together."

Sylvie thought back to their whirlwind courtship and had to admit he was right. "We spent most of our time in bed."

He grinned suddenly. "Good times."

Unsmiling, she shook her head. "That intimacy gave us a skewed sense of closeness, of connection."

"I need to move on, Sylvie." Those gray eyes were dead serious now. He extended his hand. "Do we have a deal?"

She'd made many mistakes in her life, but Andrew had been her biggest. She hadn't meant to hurt him. If spending time with her these next three weeks would help him, she'd do it.

She shook his hand and gave it a firm shake. "To-morrow, we'll begin the immersion. Tonight, I have a party to attend."

Chapter Six

Sylvie smiled when Josie skidded to a stop and gave the painting of a wild-eyed buffalo hanging on the wall of the Museum of Wildlife Art a second look.

She had to admit there was something creepy—yet compelling—about the bison's intense stare.

Josie's gaze shifted back to Sylvie. "Let me see if I've got this straight. You were once engaged to the delectable Dr. Andrew O'Shea."

Keeping the animal in her peripheral vision, Sylvie nodded.

"You broke up with him. I don't understand that, but, hey, that's your business. Then you moved here. He's making you spend the next three weeks with him so he can…" Josie's voice trailed off. "This is where you lost me."

"Andrew is convinced that the more he's around me, the more he'll discover he doesn't like me." Sylvie tried not to show how much the thought hurt. "I think he's secretly hoping he'll grow to hate me."

"Ah, the picture is coming into better focus." Josie spoke in a melodramatic tone worthy of a world-class fortune-teller. All she needed to complete the picture was a crystal ball between her fingers. "The man still has the hots for you."

"No, he…" Sylvie paused, then reluctantly admitted, "We always had chemistry."

"Do you still?"

"Uh, we can talk about that later."

"I want to talk about it now."

"Later." Sylvie ignored the pleading look in her friend's eyes. She didn't want to get into all that. Not now. Not here. "We're running low on the baked meringues."

Josie's hands, which had been clasped together, dropped to her sides. She expelled a resigned sigh and glanced at the table. "I thought you'd brought more than enough for the number they were expecting."

The linen-clad table held several varieties of petits fours. While these types of desserts didn't particularly refill Sylvie's creative well, they helped pay the bills.

Tonight, the Sweet Adelines organization was hosting an open house for prospective members. They'd rented out the museum to add a little pizzazz to their annual recruitment event.

A baby grand piano had been brought into the main room, and several members stood harmonizing around the glossy black surface. One of them was Kathy Randall, Mayor Tripp Randall's mother.

Kathy was the one who'd contacted Sylvie about catering the event. Sylvie hadn't expected Josie to volunteer to help her. Especially not with the wedding less than a month away. But Josie had insisted and Sylvie had to admit having her friend with her tonight had made the evening more enjoyable.

Josie's hand swept the room. "These women are like a swarm of locusts."

"Shhh." Sylvie elbowed her friend, but had to agree. The pastries were being consumed at an alarming rate. "I'm hoping once the singing really gets going, they'll forget chowing down and concentrate on music."

Josie shot her a pitying glance as they headed into the kitchen, where extra desserts waited. "Now, what I want to know is, since you've agreed to move into the house Andrew is renting in Spring Gulch, does that mean you're going to sleep with him?"

"Josie."

"I believe it's a valid question."

Sylvie knew she couldn't put Josie off for long, but she bought herself a little more time by filling a silver tray with several dozen baked meringues in various colors. "He's not renting the house. It belongs to a friend."

Josie followed her back into the main room. "If you think you can sidetrack me that easily, you must have had more than club soda tonight. The question on the table is, are you going to sleep with him?"

Sylvie carefully arranged the tiny bits of meringue. "Not in the plans."

"It never is." Josie's eyes took on a distant look and a little smile lifted her lips. "The last person in this whole town I planned to sleep with was Noah Anson. You see where that ended up. I can't keep my hands off him."

"And I can't keep mine off you."

The deep voice had both of them turning.

Josie giggled like a teenager surprised by her boy-friend.

Sylvie's heart dipped to her toes when she saw the man beside Noah.

For a second a nervous giggle rose in her own throat.

"What are you doing here?" Pleasure spilled from Josie's voice. "I didn't think I'd see you tonight."

Noah, looking handsome in dark pants and a muted plaid shirt, looped an arm around Josie's shoulders and tugged her to him. It was as if he couldn't bear to be so near and not touch. It had been like that for her and Andrew once, Sylvie thought wistfully.

"I ran into this guy downtown." Noah jerked a thumb in Andrew's direction. "We got to talking and decided to stop by and see if you needed help."

"Looks like a wild party." Andrew spoke for the first time since walking up.

Bits of harmony mingled with the sounds of muted laughter and conversation.

"It's a gathering of the local Sweet Adelines group," Sylvie explained. "They're wooing prospective mem-bers."

"And eating everything in sight," Josie confided.

Sylvie couldn't figure out why Andrew was here. They'd agreed to terms, one of them being they'd wait to begin the "immersion" tomorrow.

"How much longer until you're sprung?" Noah asked.

Sylvie didn't have a chance to say Josie could leave anytime when Kathy Randall rushed up. Worry fur-rowed the older woman's brow. "Do either of you ladies happen to play the piano?"

Josie shook her head. "Sorry. 'Chopsticks' is it for me."

"That's more than I can do." Sylvie touched Kathy's arm. "Is there a problem?"

"We always have a sing-along with the piano at events like these." Kathy gestured to the baby grand. "But Suzanne Duggan came down with a nasty cold today. Knowing we were counting on her, she came tonight, but we sent her home."

"There isn't anyone in your group who plays?" Sylvie found it difficult to believe there wasn't at least one person in this group of singers who could bang out a few tunes.

"We have several." Kathy's cheeks pinked. "But Suzanne has been doing this for years. She can play anything the crowd wants, so we didn't bring any sheet music."

"I can help." Andrew stepped forward, extended a hand. "I don't believe we've met. I'm Andrew O'Shea, a friend of Sylvie's."

"You play the piano, Mr. O'Shea?"

"Please call me Andrew." He flashed her the smile that had always made Sylvie go weak in the knees. "I haven't played much in recent years, but I'm proficient. I also have a good ear for music and pick up most tunes easily." Sylvie could see Kathy react to the self-assured tone. Not bragging, that wasn't Andrew's style, just confident.

Kathy surprised them all by flinging her arms around Andrew and giving him a hug. "You're a lifesaver."

"Glad to help out," Andrew said.

"Everyone," Kathy called out at the same time she motioned for him to follow her to the piano. "We've got our pianist."

Applause echoed off the walls graced by portraits of elk, bison and majestic mountains.

Josie leaned close to Sylvie. "Is he any good?"

Sylvie just smiled, not about to admit that she'd never heard him play.

Andrew sat at the piano, played a few scales with nimble fingers, then smiled up at Kathy. "What would you like me to play first?"

"Hold that thought." Kathy flashed him a smile, then whirled and clapped her hands sharply.

Several women in the back of the room immediately ceased their conversation.

"Ladies, this part of the program is a chance for us to warm up our voices and have a bit of fun doing it."

"I'll toss out the first song. The rest of you be thinking what you'd like to request next." Kathy turned to Andrew and surprised them all by requesting "Friends in Low Places."

Sylvie was shocked when Andrew's fingers settled on the keys and he began to play the country classic.

Sylvie hadn't expected to sing. She was here only to do the catering. But when Kathy looped an arm through hers and smiled, she sang along to the Garth Brooks hit.

Instead of simply following the melody, Sylvie found herself harmonizing with Kathy. The older woman's smile of pleasure encouraged her to continue.

The moment the song ended, someone in the audience requested "Country Roads." Sylvie considered stepping away to check the desserts, but decided what would be the point? Everyone at this party had forgotten all about food, except for Noah and Josie, who appeared to be doing more sampling than singing.

After a half dozen, Kathy clapped her hands once again and announced the sing-along portion of the evening had come to an end.

Andrew rose from the piano bench to a rousing chorus of applause.

When Sylvie turned, intending to check on how many desserts Josie and Noah had left, Kathy restrained her.

"You have a lovely alto, my dear. Have you thought about joining our group?"

Sylvie cocked her head. Was the woman joking?

"I believe she's serious." Andrew stepped to her side. "I heard you harmonizing. You've got a nice voice."

"I'm flattered." Sylvie shifted from one foot to the other. "But growing my business has to be my priority."

"Of course it does." Kathy nodded understandingly. "But I believe you'll discover the more involved you become in the community, the more referrals you'll receive. In Jackson Hole, who is picked to cater events is often as much a result of personal connections as it is the person's talent with food. Just think about it. You don't need to decide tonight. I'll be in touch."

"She's right, you know," Andrew said as Kathy walked away.

"I don't have time to sing." Sylvie wondered why she sounded so cross when she'd actually enjoyed the interlude. "What are you doing here, anyway?"

She'd counted on having this evening to get her head on straight. Seeing Andrew, making love with him, had thrown her off balance. Dear God, what had she been thinking?

She hadn't been thinking—that was the problem. For the past three months she'd convinced herself she was over him. Her reaction to him yesterday said that had been only wishful thinking. Getting over him was obviously still very much a work in progress.

When he'd played several love songs with those clever fingers that had played across her body less than twenty-four hours ago, her heart ached with longing for the life with him she'd once envisioned.

It wasn't fair for him to come here, all handsome and talented, and remind her of what she'd lost. But then, hadn't she learned long ago that life was seldom fair?

"This is better."

She blinked and realized he'd maneuvered her into a tiny room filled with Native American artifacts. Andrew, by his mere presence, stood so close she could smell the subtle spicy scent of his cologne and see the tiny gold flecks in his gray eyes.

"We can talk here." His gaze remained on her. "I ran into Noah downtown."

The area was so small, and for a second, Sylvie was confused. Why had he brought up Josie's fiancé? Then she realized he was explaining why he was here tonight. Or attempting to explain.

"Just because he was coming here to see Josie didn't mean you had to accompany him. Men aren't wolves. They don't run in packs."

He flashed a quick grin, seemingly not disturbed by her petulant tone. "Noah mentioned his fiancée was helping you with your catering duties this evening. He told me he planned to stop over and see if he could lend any assistance."

"Still doesn't explain your presence."

"He knew I wasn't busy. Since you and I will be seen

together in the next few weeks, I decided it might look odd if I didn't offer to come along."

As far as logical arguments went, it was a sound one.

"I didn't know you played the piano so well," she said abruptly.

"I didn't know you sang so well."

Sylvie's lips quirked. "That was a surprise, even to me."

He chuckled.

Suddenly that blasted electrical pull reared up and zapped her silly. Though she'd made it clear this "immersion" thing wouldn't include sexual contact, in a matter of hours she was tempted to break her own rule.

Andrew stepped forward. Or had she moved closer? He certainly hadn't lifted her hands to his shoulders.

"Sylvie, we're getting short of—"

Josie came to an abrupt stop. She smiled.

Behind her, Noah grinned. He surveyed the small, private alcove with an appreciative eye. "I'll have to remember this space."

Josie studied them both, a sly smile topping her lips. "If you're busy—"

Sylvie dropped her hands and stepped from Andrew, hoping the fact that her face burned didn't mean she was blushing. Why did they keep these places so blasted hot? "We're done here."

Andrew shot her a bland smile. "If there's anything I can do to help…"

"Thanks. I've got this under control." As she brushed past him and the electricity crackled, she only wished it were true.

Chapter Seven

Sylvie rose extra early the next day to bake. Since it was Labor Day, most of the restaurants, cafés and coffee shops she had contracts with had ordered extra of the cakes and pastries they normally requested. In addition, she made up little cake bites and decorated them with the Star Wars characters that were so popular now.

As Andrew hadn't made an appearance by the time the baked goods were ready to be delivered, Sylvie loaded up Ethel with bakery boxes and began her deliveries.

She wondered what had delayed him. Did it have something to do with the phone call he'd received last evening? As the Sweet Adelines event was winding down, he'd received a call from a patient back in Boston.

Sylvie told herself to relax and enjoy the morning solitude, but her thoughts kept drifting to how he'd looked at the piano, fingers flying over the keys. Then there was that "almost" kiss in the alcove…

Her thoughts were on anything but business as she made her final delivery to a local coffee shop. Hill of Beans in Jackson Hole was the only store in the coffee empire begun by Cole Lassiter where you could often find the man himself working the counter.

From what she'd heard, Cole was a local boy who'd left town with nothing but a high school education and had returned home a success. As Sylvie opened the side door, she spotted him behind the counter, coaching an obviously new employee on the fine art of making the perfect cup of cappuccino.

Cole looked up when the bells chimed. He smiled and lifted a hand in greeting. In many ways he reminded her of Andrew. Both had lean, athletic builds, dark hair and similarly shaped eyes. But there was a wariness and a hardness in Cole's eyes that said he'd survived the worst life had to offer.

Sylvie recognized the look because when she gazed into the mirror every morning, she saw that same wariness, yet Cole had climbed that steep mountain and was now happily on the other side. He was married and had two children with his wife, Meg, a physical therapist.

Sylvie had gotten to know Meg fairly well. She was one of the owners of Body Harmony Inc., the multi-therapy specialty clinic where Josie worked as a massage therapist.

Setting the tray of scones, cinnamon rolls and other goodies on the counter, Sylvie smiled at the teenage employee Cole was coaching.

Something in the girl's eyes told Sylvie this was another person who'd had a rough start in life. Sylvie wasn't surprised Cole had hired her. He was known for giving others a helping hand up.

He'd done that for her, for her business. When she'd stopped in to discuss providing the treats people loved to have with their coffee, they'd sat and talked for the longest time, simply getting acquainted. Despite the fact that she'd had bills to pay and no income at that moment, Sylvie had tried not to let her desperation show.

She remembered the strong shake of his hand when they'd come to an agreement. His kindness and faith in her were something she planned to pay forward one day.

Cole's gaze skimmed the tray's contents. He gave a nod of approval. "These look great, Sylvie."

The girl—Amber, according to her name tag—stepped forward, her brown eyes widening at the sight of all the goodies, settling on the minicakes. "You made these?"

Sylvie nodded.

"How'd you know what to do?"

She understood the puzzled look. Her mother hadn't been handy in the kitchen, either.

"I taught myself. YouTube videos, online tutorials, sites dedicated to baking. You name it, I watched or read it. I experimented. I learned what worked…and what didn't." Sylvie smiled wryly, recalling those early disasters. "After high school, I received a scholarship to a culinary institute in New York City."

A look of awe blanketed the girl's face. "You must be really smart."

"I simply loved baking." Sylvie shrugged off the praise. "Creating feeds my soul."

The girl nodded, then shifted her gaze to a spot behind Sylvie. "May I help you, sir?"

A prickle tickled Sylvie's spine. She didn't need to turn her head to know it was Andrew. If she hadn't been so focused on the conversation, on the girl's enthusiasm, she'd have felt his presence sooner.

How long had he been standing there? she wondered. Then again, what did that matter?

"I'm with her." He gestured with his head toward Sylvie.

She saw Cole's gaze sharpen and his expression turn speculative. Keeping her own expression bland, Sylvie shifted and smiled at Andrew.

When he placed a hand on her shoulder, she felt the heat of his touch all the way through the thin cotton to the skin beneath. "I got caught up on a call."

Andrew switched his focus to Cole and Amber. "Any chance we can get a couple of cappuccinos to go?"

"I believe we can manage that order." Cole smiled at his new employee. "Would you like to make them?"

The girl hesitated momentarily, then nodded.

"Just remember." Sensing Amber's uncertainty, Sylvie spoke in an encouraging tone. "Practice really does make perfect."

Amber stepped to the cappuccino machine, squared her shoulders and began to work the controls. She glanced back for a second and Sylvie shot her a wink.

When Sylvie refocused on the men, she found Cole and Andrew talking sports with an ease that surprised her. "Do you know each other?"

"I wandered in here a couple of days ago." Andrew glanced around the shop, his gaze lingering on the yellow stars plastered on the shop's windows. "I asked Cole about the interesting decor."

Sylvie had noticed the bright yellow cutouts but hadn't really paid attention to them. She stepped close for a better look. Each star contained the name of a person and "People's Health Center."

Obviously sensing her puzzlement, Cole moved to the window and plucked one of the stars. "This name represents an individual who contributed to the clinic that will serve the medically indigent in the area," he explained.

"Is that the building out on the highway?" Sylvie drove by the square, one-story building with the stone façade often. The place had been under construction since she'd arrived in Jackson Hole. "I noticed it now has a big Grand Opening sign out front."

"The grand opening is this Saturday. There will be tours and Hill of Beans will have a beverage cart in the parking lot offering free lattes and cappuccinos." A satisfied smile lifted Cole's lips. "A lot of people in Jackson Hole have worked long and hard to make this clinic a reality."

"You said something the other day about a Dr. McGregor being instrumental," Andrew prompted.

"Mitzi McGregor is an orthopedic surgeon here in Jackson. She and her husband have been pushing for this for a while now." Cole glanced at Sylvie. "When you grow up in poverty, you understand the challenges kids and adults face in obtaining even the most basic health care."

Before more could be said, Amber returned with two "go" cups. "I hope you like them."

"I'm sure we will." Impulsively Sylvie placed a hand

on the girl's shoulder. "I'm going to have you make all my drinks in the future."

Amber flushed, but Sylvie saw the words had pleased the girl.

She picked up her drink.

"If you end up running short of doctors to staff the clinic, I can function as a locum tenens while I'm here and see patients," Andrew told Cole.

Though Cole appeared to understand what that meant, Sylvie didn't have a clue. She waited until she and Andrew had stepped outside to ask him. "What does 'locum tenens' mean?"

He took her arm. "Let's go for a walk and I'll tell you."

As Hill of Beans was her final stop of the morning, there wasn't anywhere Sylvie needed to be.

"I have a license to practice medicine in Massachusetts," Andrew said as they strolled down the sidewalk. Because of the early hour, most of the businesses were still closed. "I won't be here long enough to apply for and receive a Wyoming license. Locum tenens is a way for doctors to temporarily fill in for another doctor who is unavailable, usually because of illness or vacation."

It sounded complicated to Sylvie. But as he continued to explain, she realized none of this got to the heart of what she really wanted to know. "You're here on a type of vacation. Why do you want to work?"

When his footsteps slowed, she glanced around and realized they'd reached the downtown district that edged into residential, where lawns were like carpets of green and brightly colored flowers bloomed in hanging planters from porches and around trees.

Andrew paused in front of a black fence with ornate

scrollwork that led into a small neighborhood park. "This looks like a good place to rest."

Sylvie had noticed the park before but had never been inside. There was a small play area for children boasting an old-fashioned merry-go-round, a metal slide and some rocking animals on springs.

There was also a swing set with U-shaped seats, wrought-iron benches and bushes sculpted in the shapes of various animals.

Ignoring the benches, Sylvie headed for the swings and took a seat. After a momentary hesitation, Andrew commandeered the swing closest to hers.

Dropping her bag to the ground, she sipped her cappuccino. "You haven't answered my question."

"I enjoy the practice of medicine." He took a sip from the red cup. She could tell he was pleasantly surprised by the taste when he put the cup back to his lips for a long drink. "It's hard to keep these clinics fully staffed, especially at the beginning."

"How would you know? You've never worked one before." She might have said it as a statement, assuming he was a guy whose practice catered to the wealthy, but the truth was, she didn't know if he had or not. Sylvie was beginning to realize there could be a lot about her former fiancé she didn't know.

"The first time was during a residency rotation." His gaze lifted to the sky as if he was tempted to swing for the sky. Instead he refocused on her. He said, looking oddly at ease in the swing, "Once I finished my residency and fellowship, I had to cut down to once a month because I was busy launching my concierge practice."

"Where you only see rich people."

He winced. "A practice where I've agreed to be available to patients who want their doctor available 24/7."

"What are those people doing while you're here?"

"I'm still available by phone or email. I have an associate who fills in for me." He paused, his attention diverted to a tree where a squirrel sat scolding a blue jay.

After a second, his gaze returned to her. "Concierge medicine isn't for everyone, but I like getting to know my patients. It's a very personal relationship. It also allows me to help out with the family business."

The family business, Sylvie knew, was O'Shea Sports, a huge—very profitable—conglomerate. She hadn't been surprised when she heard Franklin—Andrew's father—accuse her of being after his money.

Franklin's arguments had made a lot of sense.

For the moment Andrew's father remained at the helm of the business, but from that overheard conversation Sylvie also knew Franklin planned to eventually step aside and hand over much of his duties to his son. Despite the fact that Andrew had his own career and his sister, Corinne, had been playing an active role in the business for the past five years. The patriarchal system was alive and well in the O'Shea family.

"I'll answer calls while I'm here," he said. "It would be presumptuous to think we'd be together 24/7."

"Thank God," Sylvie muttered under her breath, although she'd never found spending time with Andrew to be a hardship. He was an intelligent man with a keen sense of humor surprisingly in sync with her own.

He grinned. "I heard that."

She merely smiled and took a sip of her drink.

"I heard what you said to Amber."

Glancing at him, she cocked her head.

"About baking being your passion, about having the urge to create, to run your own business."

"All true."

"I can't believe none of that came up when we were together." He frowned, stared down at his cup.

She downed the rest of the contents in her cup and tossed it in the trash, then returned to the swing. "We weren't together all that long. I bet you also didn't know I love to swing high."

As if to illustrate, she began to pump her legs until the swing soared so high Sylvie swore she could touch the treetops.

When she was a child, she'd often walk to a local park. It was nowhere near as nice as this one. There was no shiny black gate with gilded leaves, no carefully manicured bushes. But there had been swings and when she soared into the air she left her troubles on the ground. At least for those few minutes.

She saw Andrew toss his cup in the trash. Then he began to swing until he, too, was high in the air.

After a moment, her breath came in short puffs and she laughed with the sheer joy of the moment. When they finally slowed and stopped, it felt as if all was right with the world.

She was laughing when she rose from the swing. When she stumbled slightly, Andrew was there to steady her. She let herself fall against him, her face tilted up.

Her breath caught in her throat at the look in his eyes.

With a gentle hand he brushed a strand of hair back from her face.

Sylvie knew, as sure as she knew her own name, that Andrew was going to kiss her.

And she wasn't going to stop him.

Closing his mouth over Sylvie's sweet lips was sheer madness. That, Andrew knew with every fiber of his being. Yet he could no more stop the action from occurring than he could stop himself from breathing. He folded her into his arms and kissed those glorious lips, losing himself in the taste of her.

But when her palms rose and pushed against his chest, Andrew let his arms fall to his sides and stepped back.

In the brilliant light from the overhead sun, her lips looked as plump and full as a fresh strawberry. Her cheeks had turned a dusty shade of pink and her eyes were large and mysterious. "We agreed not to do this."

"I remember." Andrew was a smart guy. He recalled that post-sex conversation.

He'd been in full agreement with the plan to keep sex out of this immersion. Not because he didn't want to have sex with her again, but because he wondered if that had been what had caused him to fall so desperately for her back in Boston.

While he thought he'd been thinking clearly when he proposed to her, when he'd planned a life with her, the strong sexual attraction between them might have affected him more than he realized.

Andrew lifted his shoulders, let them fall. "I can't seem to keep my hands off you."

He knew what his father would say to such a statement. Franklin O'Shea was a businessman who ruled his personal and professional life strictly on logic. Andrew couldn't see his dad losing control over any-thing—or anyone—and that included Andrew's mother, his wife of forty years.

"I know." Sylvie exhaled a heavy sigh, before her lips tipped in a wry smile. "I appear to have the same problem."

"What are we going to do about it?"

"Keep working on our self-control?"

Her matter-of-fact tone made him laugh. "Sounds like a good plan."

That settled, Sylvie began walking to the park's gates. Beside her, Andrew fell into step.

"What's on tap for the rest of the day?" Back in Bos-ton, he'd been the one with the crazy schedule. Here, the situation was reversed.

"I need to start preparations for a wedding cake next weekend, but that doesn't have to be done today." When they reached the sidewalk, she turned in the direction of downtown and her shop.

"Good." Andrew couldn't recall the last time he had nothing that needed to be done. "If I wasn't here, tell me how you'd be spending your day off."

Had he ever asked her that before? It wasn't that he hadn't been interested in her life. He had been, An-drew reassured himself. It was simply that, between the business he handled for O'Shea Sports and tend-ing to patients, most of the conversations he recalled had revolved around *his* activities.

Sylvie's eyes brightened. A sudden chill settled over him. If she said "shopping" he'd stab his eye out.

"There's a nice trail in Yellowstone." Her expression gave nothing away. Yet he could feel her tension. "I like to bike. A couple of times I've even brought along some sandwiches with me and had a picnic by Jenny Lake."

In Andrew's mind, those weren't the kind of activities usually done alone. Was this her way of telling him she'd been seeing someone here in Jackson Hole? He doubted it had gone beyond casual, or the guy would be calling or texting.

"Who do you go with on these picnics?" He kept his tone as offhand as hers.

She flushed. "There's nothing wrong with spending time alone."

Her chin jutted out, daring him to say differently.

Andrew felt a surge of relief. Only because, he told himself, he didn't need to worry about some other guy wanting her attention during the next three weeks. Once Andrew returned to Boston, another guy was free to move in on her, but not before.

A tightness clenched his belly at the thought of another man doing *anything* with Sylvie, whether he was around to witness it or not.

"No," he said, "there isn't."

Her jaw relaxed.

"That's settled. We'll pick up a couple of bikes and have a picnic." Andrew glanced up at the sky. Bright blue and not a cloud in sight.

Her eyebrows pulled together. "What are you saying?"

He thought that would be evident, but he didn't mind clarifying. "I'm going with you. That's the whole point of immersion. Wherever you are, whatever you're doing, I'll be with you."

She hesitated for only a second, then shrugged.

Twenty-one days, he thought. By the time those

weeks were over, he'd know her inside and out. Then he could move on with his life, understanding that the two of them were too different to have ever stood a chance at lifelong happiness.

But as they continued down the sidewalk, he had to stop from whistling.

Chapter Eight

In the parking lot of the Jackson Hole and Greater Yellowstone Visitor Center, Sylvie helped Andrew unload the bikes. Hers was a beat-up Trek destined for the trash heap when it had been donated to the local Goodwill store.

The employees at Goodwill had done basic servicing of the bike and gotten it roadworthy. She hadn't needed a brand-new shiny one; this one would do just fine. The bike had been an impulsive purchase, bought on a day when no one was putting in orders and thoughts of Andrew had been bringing tears to her eyes.

She hadn't needed a bike, at that point couldn't really even afford one from Goodwill. Yet she'd bought it anyway. Just because her childhood hadn't been filled with bike rides and picnics didn't mean she couldn't enjoy those activities now.

From his position in the van, Andrew wheeled his bike to the back edge and she maneuvered it down to the asphalt. Like hers, his was a Trek, but this shiny black beauty was brand-new, purchased from a local bike shop the second they opened.

They'd walked in. Andrew had scanned the inventory, pointed to the top-of-the-line model and announced, "I'll take that one."

The salesclerk, a young man in his early twenties, had been eager to comply.

And now, Sylvie thought, they stood with the beauty of the Tetons surrounding.

"You could have rented a bike," she reminded him.

He shrugged, adjusted his helmet. "I'll donate it to one of the youth programs before I return to Boston."

She nodded, then reached for her own helmet. His comment was a good reminder that their time together was limited.

"Tell me again why you recommended this route?"

"It'll give us a good workout and we'll see a lot of beautiful scenery on the way." She gave her scarred and battered bike an encouraging pat, then settled on the seat. Though the day was in the sixties, she wore biker shorts and a tank under the windbreaker she planned to take off once they got started. "This trail, it's got a big fancy name, but most around here just call it the Pathway— ends at Jenny Lake. I thought we could eat our sandwiches at the lake, take a little walk and then head back."

"Why don't we just bike in Yellowstone?"

"Not a good idea. We'd have to share the roadway with cars and tourists more interested in watching out for bears than bicycles."

Andrew swung a leg over his bike, looking sexy as sin in all black.

Sylvie could tell her physical stamina had improved in the last few months when she had no difficulty keeping up with Andrew.

"I'm glad you recommended this trail," Andrew said when they paused at the bridge that passed over the scenic Gros Ventre River. "Amazing views."

"You haven't seen anything yet," she assured him as they continued on through Grand Teton National Park.

They encountered other cyclists. But for such a beautiful day, the trail was surprisingly light in traffic. They'd nearly reached Jenny Lake when they saw a man sprawled on the side of the trail, his wife bent over him, crying.

Bikes were on the ground nearby.

Andrew, Sylvie noticed, increased his speed, just as she did, to reach the couple more quickly. He hopped off his bike, reaching the couple in several long strides.

Sylvie was only several steps behind him.

"I'm a physician. What seems to be the problem?" Andrew crouched down beside the woman, who appeared to be in her late fifties.

"George was complaining that his chest hurt." The middle-aged woman looked up, her lined cheeks streaked with tears. "Are you better now, honey?" Sylvie saw horror blanket the woman's face as her fingers curved into his shirtfront. "George. George." Her head jerked up. "He's not breathing."

Andrew gently pushed her aside, checking for a pulse. His gaze met Sylvie's. "Call 9-1-1."

He began CPR. "I tried when he said his chest hurt." The woman bent over Andrew's shoulder. "But I couldn't get a signal."

"She's right," Sylvie told Andrew. "No signal. I can ride to the visitor center and—"

Another cyclist rode up just then, a young athletic man. "Problem?"

"Heart problems. CPR started," Sylvie told the guy. "We need the rescue squad but can't get a signal. The visitor center—"

"I know where it is. I'll send help." Without another word, the man jumped back on his bike and sped off.

Sylvie watched him disappear from sight before she turned to the woman, still staring wide-eyed at Andrew, as he continued to perform CPR on her unresponsive husband.

"My name is Sylvie." She moved to the woman, using what she hoped was a soothing tone. "That's Dr. O'Shea."

The woman reached out and clasped Sylvie's hands, hope in her eyes. "A medical doctor?"

"An internist." Sylvie gave the ice-cold fingers a squeeze. "Your husband couldn't be in better hands."

"I'm Barbara Williams." The woman's lips trembled. "I'm so glad you stopped. I didn't know what to do when I couldn't get a signal. I couldn't leave George, but I knew he needed help."

"If I was hurt or injured, Dr. O'Shea is the one I'd want tending to me." Sylvie maneuvered the woman over to a bench at the side of the trail. The two women sat, their hands still clasped.

Wondering where in the heck the EMTs were, Sylvie continued to speak to the woman, finding out they were tourists from Wisconsin and that George had a family history of heart disease.

She relayed the information to Andrew.

"He's breathing. His heartbeat is strong." Andrew sat back on his haunches, then restrained George as he attempted to sit up. "Easy now."

"What—what happened?" George asked in a raspy voice.

Barbara pushed to her feet and stumbled to his side, the tears beginning anew. "Oh, honey, I was so worried."

There wasn't time to say more as the EMTs were suddenly coming down the trail in a vehicle that reminded Sylvie of a toy ambulance. Andrew gave his report as two others transferred the man to a gurney. In a matter of minutes they were gone.

"Good work," Sylvie said to Andrew when they disappeared from sight.

"I heard you comforting his wife. You did good work, too." He raked a hand through his hair. "I'd say we made a good team."

Sylvie only smiled and turned to retrieve her bike. When she'd seen Andrew stop to come to the aid of a stranger, when she'd watched him continue to do CPR even after the minutes dragged on, his face a study in determination, she realized she'd been fooling herself all these months.

Sylvie had convinced herself she was over him, what she'd felt for him had been merely lust mixed with infatuation. Now she had to admit she'd been only fooling herself.

When she looked back at him, she didn't see the rich scion of a sporting-goods empire that spanned the world, or doctor who tended to the rich; she saw a caring, compassionate man.

She saw the man she'd never stopped loving.

* * *

Andrew left it up to Sylvie whether they continued to Jenny Lake or returned to Jackson. She'd been unusually quiet since the techs took George away. The entire episode had been surreal, but he was glad he'd been here. Without intervention, the man would not have survived.

"Let's head back," Sylvie said. "I feel this urge to work off some of this tension. I'm not sure a walk around a lake and a picnic are going to do it for me."

He understood. The adrenaline high he was experiencing would eventually dissipate, but for now he, too, was revved.

They rode fast and hard, covering the distance back to town in half the time of their earlier, more leisurely ride. By the time they hit the parking lot at the visitor center, the high had dissipated.

"Let's go to the house," Andrew said. "We can put our feet up, eat the sandwiches and plan our next adventure."

"Today was quite the adventure. It'll be difficult to top." Sylvie hopped off the bicycle to do a couple of stretches. "That was a fast ride back."

Concern filled his eyes. "You should have told me if you needed to slow the pace."

"I didn't want slow. I wanted hard and fast." She paused, then grinned. "Riding, that is."

He laughed. A sudden surge of wind slapped his face. It was refreshingly cool. The air here was different, with a clean freshness that was impossible to describe.

Just like the sky. He knew Montana was billed as the "big sky" state, but he swore the sky in Wyoming went on forever. Andrew knew, even if he tried to explain the difference to his friends back home, they'd never understand. He'd been the same way. After all, how could a sky be "bigger"?

But the endless sky was no longer a vivid blue. It was gray, and based on the clouds rolling in, a storm was headed their way.

By the time they got the bikes loaded, splatters of rain slapped the van's windshield. As Andrew had left his car near Sylvie's shop, they stopped there. She changed her clothes and they then drove in separate vehicles to Spring Gulch.

His friend's house was a mammoth ranch with a stone front and a three-stall garage. Andrew pushed the remote for two of the doors and they pulled inside. When the garage door lowered, the rain began in earnest.

Andrew hopped out of his car to open Sylvie's door, but she'd already stepped out. Her eyes scanned the interior of the garage, which was empty.

"It looks as if no one lives here."

"Unless it's ski season, no one does," Andrew said over his shoulder as he unlocked the door leading into the house. He stepped back and gestured her inside.

Sylvie walked down the hall, past the laundry room and a bathroom, then stopped and stared. This place was bigger than the Teton Village condo where they'd stayed when they came to Jackson to ski. Lots bigger.

Andrew paused beside her. In front of them was the great room with soaring ceilings and a row of floor-to-ceiling windows that offered an amazing view of the Tetons. The house had an open floor plan with a well-stocked country kitchen with both a breakfast bar and a small eating area. The great room was his favorite in the house, with its stacked stone fireplace and rugged wooden mantel.

As rain continued to pelt the windows, Andrew decided that despite the earlier sixty-degree temperature, tonight he was going to enjoy a glass of wine in front of a fire.

He was contemplating the pleasure of it when he realized Sylvie still hadn't spoken. "Is something wrong?"

"It's so, so big."

For a second he thought she was joking. Then he saw the awed look in those violet eyes.

If she thought this place was big, what must she have thought of his parents' home with its suites of rooms and formal gardens? He recalled how she'd never seemed to fully relax when they were together there.

At the time, he'd attributed her unease to the fact that she hadn't known his parents well and possibly sensed their silent disapproval. But now he realized it had been more.

The house had been too big, too different from her normal world, for her to be able to relax. Because he'd been caught up with his practice and his father's attempts to involve him even more deeply in the business, he hadn't done enough to make her feel at home.

But they were alone in this house. He could make her comfortable here. Sylvie had to feel safe to let down her guard. Only then would he be able to truly get to know her.

She appeared ready to relax. When they'd stopped at her place, she changed into leggings with boots and a top with jagged edges around the hem that brought to mind Robin Hood and his merry men.

The color was an eye-popping purple that brought out the violet in her eyes. She blinked those big, beautiful eyes and cocked her head. Lifting the sack with the sandwiches they'd picked up at Hill of Beans and planned to eat at Lake Jenny, she smiled. "I don't know about you, but I'm starved. Are you ready to eat?"

"Right after I get a fire going."

"It was sixty degrees this morning." The wind punctuated her words by slapping a wall of water against the windows with the force of a hurricane blast. Sylvie appeared to reconsider. "On second thought, a fire sounds fabulous."

"There's a bottle of wine on the counter." He gestured to the bottle sitting on the granite countertop. "I'll pour us a glass after I get this fire going."

With the help of a gas starter, a fire soon blazed in the hearth. When Andrew turned, he found Sylvie standing there, a glass of wine in each hand.

Behind her, on the coffee table, were two plates holding sandwiches, cut-up fruit and chips.

Taking the glass of wine she extended, Andrew surprised himself—and her—by leaning forward and brushing her cheek with his lips. "Thanks."

He wasn't sure what made him do it, other than he and Sylvie had always been affectionate with each other.

Bright pink flared in her cheeks, but she said nothing, only took a seat on the overstuffed leather sofa facing the fire. Tucking a foot beneath her, she peered at him over her glass.

Though there was lots of space on the large sofa, Andrew sat beside her.

"What?" he asked, seeing a question in her eyes.

Sylvie cocked her head. "I have a question for you."

He sipped his wine, waited.

"What are we going to do now?"

Chapter Nine

Sylvie wasn't sure what made her ask what was next, especially in a tone that had a hint of flirtation. That was the opposite of the cool, keep-your-hands-to-yourself persona she hoped to portray.

Andrew twirled the wineglass back and forth between his fingers, the glow from the fireplace making the red liquid shimmer. "We could, oh, I don't know, talk about our day?"

"The day we spent together?"

"There hasn't been much opportunity for us to discuss what happened on the trail." His gaze shifted to the fire and his expression turned solemn. Then he appeared to blink away the clouds and shifted slightly in his seat to face her. "You kept your cool."

Sylvie experienced a flush of pleasure. "I didn't do anything. You are the one who saved George's life."

"Keeping his wife calm allowed me to tend to her husband without any distractions. Thank you."

"She was so worried about him."

"Of course. He was her husband."

"I don't believe my parents ever cared about each other like that."

He reached forward and grabbed the plate she'd fixed, his gaze never wavering from her face. He washed a bite of the ham sandwich down with a sip of wine. "You once told me your father left when you were very young."

Sylvie wondered how they'd gotten on the topic of her parents. She never liked thinking about them, much less talking about them. They were her past. She preferred looking ahead.

Yet Andrew was staring at her so expectantly she offered a resigned sigh and answered, "Though I was only four, I remember him. I remember when he used to lift me up on his shoulders so I could touch the ceiling of our apartment."

"Is that all you recall?"

"He and my mom fought all the time. Yelling and screaming and blaming each other about everything. Even when I hid between my bed and the wall and put my hands over my ears, I could still hear them fighting."

His gaze sharpened. "Did either of them ever hit you?"

Sylvie shook her head. She'd had it good there. She'd never been physically abused. "It scared me when they yelled. I think that's probably the reason I shy away from conflict."

He took another bite of the sandwich, his gaze thoughtful. "Tell me what else you remember about him."

"Well, he ate breakfast one day, went to work and never came back." She kept her tone matter-of-fact. The man had left a long time ago. She rarely thought of him anymore.

"Did he ever call?"

"Nope." Sylvie let the delicious wine settle in her mouth before she swallowed. She slipped off her boots, then propped her feet up on a leather hassock. The fire warmed the undersides of her stockinged feet.

"Do you know where he is now, or what he's doing?" Andrew pressed.

Apparently in his world people didn't simply vanish.

"Never heard and not interested." Sylvie remembered her mother crying, the initial worry that something bad had happened. Then the explosive anger when an uncaring cop had told her mother it wasn't illegal for a man to walk away from a bad marriage.

"The night before he left, I pestered him to play with me, but he brushed me off." She stared into the burgundy liquid. "They'd been fighting a lot and I think he was just tired of both her and me. I could be a real pain."

Andrew lifted the glass of wine to his lips, but instead of drinking, he only gazed at her over the rim. "Your mother did the same thing to you when you were a teenager."

The smile that lifted Sylvie's lips held no humor. "I was thirteen. She waited until after supper to leave. She'd been acting strangely—"

"How?" Andrew leaned forward, his gaze focused on her face. "How was she acting strangely?"

Sylvie thought back to that time when she'd foolishly thought life couldn't get any worse. They'd been living in a run-down apartment in Newark. Food had been in short supply. The landlord had been a frequent visitor that summer, demanding rent money.

Still, in her world none of that was unusual. Many of her friends were in the same boat. Her mother had been more interested in her boyfriends than what her teenage daughter had been doing. They'd gotten along just fine.

But there had been something in the air that last week before her mother took off. Sylvie had been worried, though she hadn't been able to pinpoint why.

She blinked and realized that Andrew was waiting for an answer. "My mother always had a lot of boyfriends."

"She and your dad divorced."

Sylvie shook her head. "She didn't have money for a divorce. She told everyone he was dead. That's what she considered him to be."

When Andrew spoke, his tone held heavy condemnation that he didn't bother to conceal. "She picked one of her boyfriends over you. She left you alone."

The words punched like a direct blow to the heart. For years, when Sylvie thought back to the time, it was always about her mother taking off. But that phrasing skirted a very important truth.

Her mother had left her.

There was no getting around that fact. The woman had left just as her dad had done. Without one word of explanation. Neither of them had cared about her enough to stay or even to leave a note of explanation.

She'd done the same to Andrew.

When he started to speak, she held up a hand. "It's not necessary to mention the connection between what they did to me and what I did to you. I get it. And I regret it. Sincerely."

Andrew's shoulders were stiff against the back of the cushions.

Sylvie continued. "My parents knew me as well as any people on this earth. I believe in their own way they loved me. But they were also aware of my strengths and my weaknesses. In the long run, what they saw in me, what they felt for me, wasn't enough to make them stay."

"You believe I'd have eventually left you, too."

"Of course." Her heart swelled in her chest. She forced herself to breathe. "Your father was right. It would only be a matter of time."

"My fath—"

"Everyone who knew, when they met me, saw us as an unlikely match." She plunged forward, not about to take a side trip to discuss his dad's very logical concerns. "You realized that, too, after I'd been gone awhile. That's the reason you're here now. You know that once you get to know the real me, you'll be able to accept that you dodged a bullet, that I did you a favor."

He opened his mouth, then shut it, took a drink of wine.

"I admit that, maybe because of my past, I'm not as open as I should be. That hesitation to let someone fully into my life extended to my relationship with you." Sylvie clasped her hands in her lap to still their trembling.

Feeling as if she were about to plunge over the side of a cliff, she took a deep breath and took the leap. "I will let you into my world, Andrew. I owe you that. The woman you'll get to know over the next few weeks will be me, no subterfuge, without artifice."

Her gaze searched his face. "That way, when you board that plane back to Boston, you'll be able to leave in peace, knowing that whoever you thought you loved, it wasn't me."

Andrew was sieged with an almost overwhelming desire to pull Sylvie into his arms and hold her close. He longed to murmur sweet words of reassurance in her ears. But that wouldn't be fair to her or to him. And it made absolutely no sense.

This was the woman who'd walked out on him. Who, by her own admission, had never looked back. If he hadn't sought her out, he knew as sure as he knew his own name they'd still be apart. Those weren't the actions of a woman in love. Those weren't the actions of the woman he thought he'd loved.

"I appreciate that," he heard himself say. "To be fair, though you've already concluded whatever you felt for me wasn't love, I promise to also fully be myself when I'm with you."

It seemed only fair.

"I hate opera."

Andrew blinked.

Her chin lifted in what could only be described as a defiant tilt. "I said I'd be honest. I might as well start now."

Taken aback by the statement, Andrew took a moment to add another log to the fire, then refilled their wineglasses before resuming his seat.

"I know most people in your social circle adore the opera and the symphony, too. Neither does anything for me." Though she spoke casually, bright patches of color dotted her cheeks and that chin remained stubbornly lifted. "I tried. I was bored."

Andrew had taken her to the Boston Opera House several times when they were together. Up to this moment, he'd have sworn she'd enjoyed the evenings. "There wasn't *anything* you liked about the performances?"

Instead of being offended, he found himself intrigued. Getting this glimpse inside her head was fascinating.

She thought for a moment, took a bite of sandwich, then washed it down with a sip of wine.

"I thought the opera house was incredibly beautiful. I loved the soaring ceiling, the columns with the gold leaf finishes and all the marble." Her eyes took on a distant glow, as if she was looking back, remembering those evenings with the promise of summer in the air. "The chandeliers were breathtaking, and when the place was filled with all those beautiful people, well, all that stuff made sitting through the performances bearable."

Andrew finished off his sandwich, finding the sound of rain pattering on the roof oddly soothing. Someone, either he or Sylvie, had turned on a light, and now, because of the darkening skies outside, the lamp bathed the room in a golden glow.

The area where they sat had turned suddenly small, almost as if their world had shrunk and they were the only ones in this warm little cocoon, where secrets could be freely shared.

"You liked the surroundings but didn't like the opera or the symphony." Andrew kept his tone conversational.

She nodded.

"What about the ballet?" They'd attended a performance of *Swan Lake*. Again, he thought she'd enjoyed it but now, thinking back, he wasn't so sure. Each time his gaze had strayed from the stage to her, she was glancing around the concert hall.

"Not really." She lifted her shoulders, let them fall. "Perhaps if I'd had some exposure to ballet as a child, I'd have a greater appreciation for all the moves, but—"

"Not your thing," he said.

"Not my thing." The words came out on a sigh. She took another sip of wine and her gaze shifted to the fire.

"Why didn't you tell me how you felt?" Again, he strove for conversational, truly wanting to understand.

She shifted her attention back to him. "You were so excited to show me your world. I wanted to explore. I told myself to give them a chance. I hoped that opera and ballet and all that stuff would grow on me once it became more familiar."

"It didn't."

"It hadn't…but that's not to say it wouldn't have, given time." She gave a rueful smile. "I'd planned to do some outside studying so I could appreciate it. Maybe even take a ballet class or two. But between the time we spent together and my baking, there never seemed to be any extra time."

"Why bother at all?"

Her gaze met his. "You enjoyed it. You were important to me. I wanted the love of these kinds of things to be something we could share."

The sentiment spoke to a generosity of spirit. It also made him wonder what would have happened if there had been something in her world that she'd liked and he didn't. Would he have been so generous? It was a sobering thought and one he wasn't ready to explore.

His lips quirked up. "Anything else you particularly hated?"

"I didn't ha—"

"I'm teasing." Andrew reached over and covered her hand with his. "Thank you for being honest."

"I should have told you at the time."

"You're telling me now."

Without warning she slipped her hand from his and rose to her feet. She didn't speak, merely strode to the panes of glass now experiencing the full force of the storm's wrath.

She was slender as a willow and so…alone.

He fought the urge to go to her now, to wrap his arms about her in comfort. The realization stirred something inside him.

Andrew pushed to his feet, quickly moving across the shiny hardwood to where she stood. When he wrapped his arms around her, Sylvie stiffened. After a moment she relaxed against him, her body soft against his.

"I wasn't going to do this," he said, his voice a soft, low rumble.

"Do what?" she whispered back, making no move to turn around.

"Come to you, comfort you." He expelled a breath. "But I'd promised to be genuine during these weeks together and I—I wanted to hold you."

"I'm glad you did." Her voice was so soft he barely heard her. "I believe this forced interaction is going to be harder on us than we think."

"It may be difficult." Andrew dropped his head forward so his chin rested on the top of her head. "Still, in the end, when the three weeks is up, we'll know we made a grand effort."

Chapter Ten

Sylvie moved into the large house that evening. Andrew wanted to come with her to pick up her things, but she told him it'd be easier for her to go through her stuff alone. When he received another call about his patient in Boston, she slipped out of the house, his car keys in hand.

Her van was back in Jackson and, for now, that was where it would remain. She would pick up a few personal items that she'd need, along with some clothes, and call it good.

The trip into town took less time than she anticipated. It would probably be super quick at 3:00 a.m. when she left to do her baking. Perhaps living in Spring Gulch for the next few weeks wouldn't be that bad.

The home was beautiful and she enjoyed the warmth of the fireplace this evening. Still, it wouldn't do to get too comfortable. Once Andrew left she'd be back in her "Spartan" digs. It'd be a long time before she could afford anything better.

The rain was coming down in a steady stream and she was grateful when the garage door slid open and she could pull her vehicle inside. She was still slightly damp from her dash into her shop when the rain was at its worst.

Andrew looked up from his laptop when she walked into the kitchen. In the time that she'd been gone, he'd changed into jeans and a charcoal shirt. "Sounds like the rain is coming down at a good clip."

"Forget rain. Think typhoon." Sylvie dropped the single battered suitcase on the floor. "Did you get your patient on the road to recovery?"

Gentleman that he was, Andrew pushed back his chair and stood. He glanced at the scarred suitcase and crossed the room. "I'll get the other bags out of the car."

"There are no other bags."

He whirled, obviously trying to control his surprise. "Seriously?"

"That's all I have." She chuckled. "And all I need."

His gaze dropped to the case, the size of an airline carry-on, before refocusing on her. "You believe in traveling light."

"Something like that." Sylvie meandered across the shiny floor to the cupboards. "Do you mind if I get myself something to drink?"

"Mi casa su casa."

She'd just opened the refrigerator when the doorbell rang. Sylvie cocked her head. "Are you expecting someone?"

"No. You?" Andrew tossed the words over his shoulder on his way to the front door.

"No one but Josie knows I'm here," she called after him.

Curious, Sylvie decided to check it out for herself.

Andrew shook his head, his body between her and the unexpected visitor.

Sylvie saw by the look on his face that he didn't recognize the man at the door. Instead of using an umbrella to ward off the rain, the tall, broad-shouldered man had simply pulled up the hood of his jacket.

"I know we haven't met. I'm—" The visitor paused, catching sight of Sylvie. "Now, there's someone familiar. Hi, Sylvie."

"Hi, Keenan." Sylvie smiled and motioned him inside. "Don't just stand there. Come in out of the rain."

Andrew stepped aside to let Keenan inside, then closed the door behind him.

Keenan pushed back his hood. For a second Sylvie thought he was going to shake off like a wet dog. He paused and appeared to think better of it. Still, he wiped a hand against his jeans before extending his hand to Andrew. "I'm Keenan McGregor, your neighbor."

"Andrew O'Shea." Andrew took his hand, offered a smile. "My friend Jack owns this home. I'm staying here for a couple of weeks."

"It appears you've already met the best baker in the Hole." Keenan winked at Sylvie.

"That's very sweet. Thanks, Keenan."

Andrew's gaze shifted between the two of them. Whatever he saw must have reassured him because he smiled. "Can I offer you a beer? Or a soft drink?"

"Actually, I came over to issue a last-minute invitation to a small neighborhood party Mitzi and I are hosting this evening."

"Mitzi?"

"My wife."

A thoughtful look blanketed Andrew's face. "Dr. Mitzi McGregor?"

Keenan's smile remained on his lips, but his gaze had turned watchful. "You know my *wife*?"

Keenan reminded Sylvie of a coiled viper ready to strike. Though he'd always been perfectly nice to her, in that moment Sylvie could believe the rumors that he'd spent time in prison were true.

"I heard your wife is the force behind the People's Health Center."

The tension seemed to leave Keenan's shoulders and he rocked back on his heels. "It's a project that has been close to her heart—and to mine—for a number of years. We can't wait for it to open."

"Andrew is also a physician." Sylvie tossed that comment out there, though she wasn't sure why.

Keenan didn't appear impressed.

"They're everywhere in Jackson Hole." Keenan's expression looked pained. "Can't put your foot down without stepping on one."

To Sylvie's surprise, Andrew laughed. "What time is the party?"

"Seven. Wear what you have on." Their visitor gestured with one hand to his jeans and boots. "I'm not changing."

Sylvie stepped forward. "Can I bring something?"

"Just yourself." The smile Keenan bestowed on her

was warm before he turned back to Andrew. "Good to meet you, O'Shea."

Without ceremony, Keenan flipped up his hood and headed back into the rain.

"I didn't get his address." Andrew's hand moved to the doorknob, but Sylvie grabbed his arm.

"I know where they live. Mitzi had me bake a cake for Keenan's birthday last month. You should have seen it."

"What did it look like?"

"Let's just say it involved a propeller-driven plane made out of fondant and a *Mad Max* theme." Her lips curved as she recalled the three-layer cake. "The plane took the most time."

"Plane?" Andrew inclined his head. "Is Keenan a pilot?"

Sylvie nodded, even as she wondered if what she had on really was adequate or if she should change.

"You made me a Spamalot cake for my birthday," he said.

"I remember." Her smile faded as she also remembered the look of horror on Andrew's mother's face when she'd caught sight of the cake. Pushing the image aside, Sylvie slid the phone from her pocket and looked at the time. "It's already six. I'm going to unpack and then freshen up."

"If you need to know where anything is, just ask. I can't guarantee I'll know where it's at, but we can search together."

"Sounds good." She waved him away when he reached for her bag. "Seriously, I've got it."

As Sylvie made her way down the hall to where she assumed the bedrooms were located, she realized for the next three weeks she'd know exactly where Andrew was and he'd know the same about her.

She only wondered why the thought didn't bother her.

It wasn't until the evening was winding down that Andrew had the opportunity to speak privately with Mitzi McGregor. She was a pretty woman with hair the color of peanut butter and bright blue eyes.

Instead of jeans, she wore a long flowing skirt in an odd patchwork pattern with a formfitting top the color of buttermilk. Dangly earrings of the sun and moon hung from her ears and cowboy boots with a turquoise pattern completed the image.

She didn't look like an orthopedic surgeon, and he'd known plenty. But there was an intelligence in her eyes that belied the boho-chic appearance. Sylvie appeared to like her, if the big hug the two women had exchanged when they arrived was any indication.

Andrew supposed he and Sylvie should head home. But Sylvie seemed so relaxed and happy this evening he'd decided why rush off? It wasn't as if he had anywhere to go.

Other than getting up at 3:00 a.m. to drive into Jackson… He shoved the thought aside. If she wasn't worried about the lack of sleep, he wouldn't worry, either.

"How are you enjoying your vacation?" Benedict Campbell dropped into a nearby chair that also faced the flickering flames of the fireplace.

Andrew looked up and took the bottle of beer his friend held out. He brought it to his lips and took a sip. "I'm not used to being idle."

"It would drive me crazy." Benedict grinned. "It would drive my father even crazier."

Andrew smiled. He recalled Ben talking about his father, John, and thinking he and Franklin O'Shea had a lot in common. "My father can't understand why I'm here and not spending these last few weeks in Tahiti."

Ben inclined his head. "Last few weeks before what?"

"I'm going to be taking more of an active role in the company business."

"Why?"

"Good question."

"What about medicine?"

"It'll go on the back burner."

Before Andrew could say more, Mitzi sashayed over—that really was the only way to describe how she walked—and took a seat on the arm of Andrew's chair.

"What's this I hear about you offering to help out at People's?"

"If you need another doctor to fill in occasionally, I'm available." Out of the corner of his eye, Andrew saw Sylvie wander over to stand by the hearth, a drink in her hand. "I know how crazy those first couple of weeks can be. It's as if the floodgates have opened. The patient volume is difficult to predict, but it's usually way over what you anticipate. If that occurs, don't hesitate to call me."

A speculative gleam filled Mitzi's eyes. "Sounds as if you've been involved in something like this before."

"Similar, but ours were what we called 'pop-up' clinics. The location of the clinics would vary. Most often we'd use church basements." Andrew took a long drink from his beer. "We enlisted a lot of medical students to help out. Working the clinic gave them some good experience as well as showed the need that is out there."

Andrew sensed Sylvie's gaze on him but stayed focused on Mitzi.

"We had some of those kinds of clinics in the neighborhood where I grew up," Mitzi said.

"I wished we'd had some of those around here when I was young." Keenan, who'd just stridden over with Poppy Campbell, positioned himself behind his wife. He rested his hands lightly on her shoulders and she leaned her head against his well-muscled, tanned arm.

Andrew had thought the couple was so different, but he now questioned his assessment. It appeared Mitzi and Keenan had more in common than he'd first thought, at least in terms of early-life experiences.

He wondered if Sylvie was looking at them, and thinking it only confirmed she'd made the right decision to leave. After all, her early background and his couldn't be more different.

"There is definitely a need here." Poppy's expression grew pensive. "Just like there was in New York City, when I lived there. Poverty is everywhere, although often those with money and power like to pretend it doesn't exist."

"You're a social worker." Andrew hoped he'd gotten that correct. He'd met so many people since his arrival in Jackson Hole that who they were and their occupations had become somewhat of a jumbled mess in his head.

Poppy smiled. "That's right. I work part-time for Teton County now. Once our baby is born—she'll be our second—I'll use my skills to help those who visit the People's Health Center on a volunteer basis."

"My wife, the radical." The teasing note in Ben's voice surprised Andrew. He remembered Benedict Campbell well from prep-school days. Andrew wasn't certain if it was maturity or if Poppy deserved the credit for the change, but his old friend was definitely mellower.

"Helping people in need shouldn't be considered a radical concept." Sylvie had wandered over to catch the last of Ben's comment. She flushed when every eye turned in her direction. "It's just the thing to do."

Just the thing to do.

By the time they left the McGregor home, the rain had stopped and the air held that clean, fresh scent of flowers and earth.

When Sylvie slipped, he grabbed her arm and then tucked it through his for the rest of the walk home.

"I realized something tonight," he said as they stood on the front porch and pulled out the key.

She stifled a yawn with her hand. "What is that?"

He stepped aside to let her enter first, then reached around her to flip the switch and flood the entryway with light. "We'd never been at a party together where we both had a good time."

"What makes you think I had a good time?"

"Did you?"

She smiled. "I did. I like Keenan and Mitzi and most of the people there."

"I enjoyed their company, too." *And yours*, he thought, but didn't say.

A clock somewhere in the house began to chime. Sylvie pulled out her phone and glanced at the time, then back at Andrew. Her lips twisted in a wry smile. "I have to be up in three hours."

He'd have to be up as well. After all, a promise was a promise.

Except when it wasn't, he thought, recalling how she'd left him. Still, he gave in to the impulse. Without considering the wisdom of what he was about to do, he leaned over and pressed his lips to hers in a sweet, gentle kiss. "Good night, Sylvie. See you in three."

Andrew sensed her eyes on him as he headed down the hall to the room he'd commandeered as his. He'd surprised her. That was good. But the victory was a hollow one. Because he was headed to his bedroom to sleep…alone.

While Sylvie added ingredients, put sheets of pastry items in the ovens and set trays to the side to cool, Andrew remained at the small table, eyes focused on his laptop.

He'd offered to help and actually had been rather persistent about it, but she'd told him she had a routine, and having a helper, even a handsome one, would disrupt her rhythm.

She wasn't sure why she'd added the *handsome* part, except maybe because she sensed he really *had* wanted to help. The comment had brought a smile to his lips.

While she'd turned on the ovens, he'd powered up his laptop. Fifteen minutes ago, he'd risen from the rickety chair and moved to the ancient Mr. Coffee machine she'd picked up for a song at the big-box store out on the highway. The delicious aroma of coffee soon mingled pleasantly with the sugar and cinnamon scents.

He brought her a cup once it was brewed, black, just the way she liked it.

After sliding a tray of scones into the oven, she accepted the chipped mug, curving her fingers around the warmth. A long sip jolted the last of the fatigue straight out of her system.

Sylvie smiled at him. Despite almost no sleep, he looked rested and alert. "I could get used to having you around."

The instant the words left her lips, Sylvie wished she could pull them back. "I mean—"

His hand closed over her shoulder, gently kneading the knots he found there. "Don't apologize. I understand what you meant."

He wandered around the small windowless room. "Sometimes it's nice to have someone around."

Sylvie set down her cup and added some sugar to a huge mixing bowl. She considered his response and her own.

"I admit I was worried how these next three weeks would go." She opened the huge refrigerator to retrieve some butter. "I've gone solo for a long time."

Inclining his head, Andrew took a long drink from his mug. "We were together, not that long ago," he reminded her.

"When you were free and when I was. We spent time together, sure." She sighed. "Often it felt as if we were two ships passing in the night. At least to me."

"I had my practice." Though his voice remained easy, there was also a defensive edge.

"Understood." She kept her tone equally offhand. "I had my work. When we were together, everything was fast-paced because it was shiny and new."

"I don't—"

"Just like when you flew me to Jackson Hole on your family's corporate jet for a weekend." The mixer creamed the butter soft as velvet before she added it to the bowl. "That trip was like something out of a fairy tale."

They'd stayed at a lodge right by the slopes. March had been snowy and there had been a lot of fresh powder. Andrew had taught her to ski during the day, while the evenings had been spent making love in front of a roaring fire.

"But the sheen didn't last."

When she blinked and refocused, Andrew was standing in the doorway, coffee mug in hand, studying her.

"I cared for you."

"Not enough."

Saved by the oven ding. Grateful for the distraction, Sylvie grabbed oven mitts and opened the mammoth door, noting with approval the golden brown of the scones. With quick, expert movements, she removed the trays and set them aside to cool, then slid several pans of brownies inside and shut the door.

It wasn't until she'd reset the oven timer that she shifted her attention back to Andrew. His gray eyes had gone cool, his expression implacable.

She resisted the urge to cross her own arms across her chest. The promise she'd given, to be honest about her feelings, chafed, but she would hold herself to it. "It was just so difficult to believe."

"What?" he asked when she refocused on the mixing bowl, instead of finishing the thought. "What was so difficult to believe?"

There was frustration simmering in the tone, and

when she heard his footsteps cross the room, Sylvie wasn't surprised.

"What is difficult to believe?" he repeated.

He wasn't going to let this go, she knew. And she'd brought this upon herself by tossing out such a cryptic comment.

Because he stood so close, Sylvie turned slightly then lifted her hand to gently pat his cheek. "It's difficult for me to believe that what is good in my life at one moment isn't going to turn bad in the next."

Chapter Eleven

By the time Friday rolled around, Andrew realized he was no closer to cracking the mystery that was Sylvie Thorne than he'd been when his plane landed in Jackson Hole. The one thing he'd learned was she had incredible stamina.

After a couple of days of getting up at three, he'd been ready to tell her to go ahead without him. He could sleep in and they could be together after she'd made her deliveries. Pride wouldn't let him take that easy way out.

Andrew had to admit the woman had a strong work ethic. And she truly had a knack for baking. Her real love definitely was cakes. The more leeway she was given in the creation, the more she appeared to enjoy the process.

So, in a way he *had* come to know her a little better. Her remark about expecting things that were going good to turn bad still nagged at him. As he pushed the door open and stepped into Hill of Beans, he found himself trying to put the puzzle pieces together in his head.

She was with her friend Josie now. The wedding was in two weeks and the bridesmaids were getting together with the bride-to-be for lunch at M. K. Fisher's house. Someone named Lexie Delacourt was responsible for the food, but Sylvie had insisted on making the cake.

Early in the week, she'd fretted—there was no other word for it—over the design. She wanted it to be something light and fun that would reflect Noah and Josie's courtship. Andrew had chuckled when he saw the finished product.

Apparently Josie had once mentioned she loved flamingos. The result was a flamingo-inspired cake complete with the bird on top wearing a tiny veil.

After making the deliveries, they'd gone back to the house so she could get ready for the party. Andrew's mother had been very social, and he couldn't count the number of society luncheons she'd attended.

He'd been unable to hide his surprise when Sylvie came out of her bedroom—the room right next to his—wearing a straight skirt and a simple sleeveless top. No pearls or other jewelry. No heels.

Though he didn't say a word, she could now read his expressions with pinpoint accuracy. She smiled. "This isn't Boston."

"I don't know what you mean." He forced an innocent look that, of course, didn't fool her.

"The instant you saw me, you were thinking this would not be appropriate in Boston."

How could he deny it? Besides, they had promised

to keep it honest. "My mother and even my sister always looked like they were going to a fashion show."

"That's the great thing about life in Wyoming." Sylvie glanced at her phone, then had sat down, apparently deciding she had some time to kill. "It's more relaxed. Mitzi will be there. She's as likely to show up in a pair of skinny jeans as a dress. Cassidy Duggan—you may have seen her at the barbecue—well, you never know what she's going to show up wearing."

The smile that lifted Sylvie's lips eased some of Andrew's worry. He always thought she looked beautiful; he just hadn't wanted her to feel awkward.

"I'm a part of this community," she said.

"In a way you never did in Boston."

He half expected her to disagree, though he knew if she did it would be a lie. At the few events they'd attended together, he'd sensed her unease. Though, at least in his earshot, everyone had been friendly and polite, she'd been an outsider in a social circle that prized connections. Not only hadn't she attended Miss Porter's or gone on to Mount Holyoke, but her family had zero social standing.

Even her award-winning cake designs weren't something that was readily admired. He couldn't imagine any of the Beacon Hill matrons serving a cake with a skull or a flamingo.

"I need to dash."

Andrew didn't know what to think when she leaned over and brushed a kiss across his cheek, before leaving.

He could have stayed home, but after a half hour decided to get out and go…somewhere. Andrew ended up at Hill of Beans.

If his friends in Boston could see him now, spending time in a coffee shop with yellow stars in the window... Even as the thought made his lips quirk up, he lifted a hand in greeting to Cole Lassiter. Yes, his friends would be shocked to see how he was spending the last weeks before assuming the COO position at O'Shea Sports.

They'd never understood why he'd gone to medical school, why he'd practiced medicine instead of moving up the ranks at the family company. Especially after his brother, who'd been groomed for that top spot, had been killed in a car accident.

Andrew pulled his thoughts back to the present. As he stepped to the counter, he eyed the bake case, pleased to see that Cole's customers had made a visible dent in the baked goods he and Sylvie had dropped off that morning.

"In the mood for some lunch or is it just coffee today?" Cole asked.

"I'll have a—" Andrew studied the menu board "—chicken salad on wheat."

"I'll get it for him." Amber smiled at Andrew, then turned toward the back counter.

"Thanks, Amber." Cole studied Andrew for a moment. "Got big plans for the afternoon?"

"Not really," Andrew said, embarrassed by the admission.

"Interested in checking out the clinic?" Cole asked. "I was going to stop over there for a few minutes and make sure everything is ready for tomorrow's grand opening."

"I'd like to see it." Andrew accepted the sandwich, ordered an iced tea to go with it. But when he pulled out his credit card, he was surprised when Cole waved away payment.

"It's on me." Cole grinned. "I'm feeling generous today."

Cole pulled up a chair and kept Andrew company while he ate. Then they rode together out to the highway.

"I see you've got Ethel today," Cole commented as he climbed into the van.

"Ethel?"

"Mary Karen Fisher—she's the one hosting the luncheon today—she gave this very same van that name years ago." Cole sniffed the air. "Sure does smell good in here."

Andrew nodded and fastened his seat belt. The van might be on its last legs, but because of all the bakery products it hauled every day, he doubted there was a sweeter-smelling car in all of Jackson Hole. "Back to Ethel."

"Oh, yeah. Well, when Mary Karen was expecting baby number five…or was it six? Anyway, they traded in Ethel and got a new Odyssey." Cole grinned. "It went through a couple of owners in the meantime, but when Sylvie showed up driving it, we recognized Ethel immediately."

"You seem to know everyone in Jackson Hole," Andrew commented.

"I grew up here, run a business here, as does my wife." Cole's tone was matter-of-fact. "I'd say between us, we know a considerable number of people."

"Sylvie likes it here." There was a hint of bitterness in Andrew's tone he didn't quite understand.

"What's not to like?" The coffee magnate grinned

and then pointed. "Turn at the next light to the left. We can park around back."

Andrew maneuvered the van into the turn lane and stopped, waiting for the green. Though the traffic appeared heavier than it had the past few days, it was nothing compared to I-93. Oddly, while he'd always enjoyed the fast pace, he found he didn't miss it. Or hadn't, he qualified. Give him three weeks and he might be yearning for a good old-fashioned traffic snarl.

The light changed and in seconds he wheeled the van around back, pulling in between two recently painted white lines. The building was attractive with its cream-colored stucco and beltline stone facade. Bushes and flowers flanked the perimeter.

As he strolled up, Andrew took note of the quality construction. Whoever built it hadn't gone overboard, but neither had they scrimped. The result was a building built to last, one that would survive the harsh winters, the driving rains and vicious winds off the Tetons. "Who was the builder?"

He wasn't sure why he asked; it wasn't like he was in the market for a contractor, but he was curious.

"Joel Dennes." Cole pulled out a ring of keys from his pocket. "You met him at Ben and Poppy's barbecue."

Andrew was this close to telling Cole he'd met a lot of people at that party when an image of a rugged man with a deep voice and stern features popped into his head. "Was he the one whose wife is the pediatrician?"

"That'd be Kate. Yep, that's the one." Cole stuck the key he'd been searching for into the lock, then pulled the door open, motioning Andrew inside.

That everything was new and shiny was his first

impression. Even the linoleum floor had been polished to a high sheen. Though Andrew preferred the look of wood, he understood the choice of floor tile. Bodily fluids would be easy to clean up on such a surface.

"You were a personal doctor to the rich," Cole commented, flipping on more lights.

"I was a concierge physician," Andrew qualified, refusing to become defensive. "My patients wanted a doctor they could call anytime. They knew when they went into the hospital I'd be the one they'd see, not some hospitalist."

"That's what I said," Cole said with a grin. "Doctor to the rich."

Andrew shook his head and laughed.

"Do you miss the variety?"

Following Cole down the hall, looking into exam rooms and conference rooms, admiring the new radiology equipment and treatment rooms, he gave the question more consideration than his guide likely expected.

"Sometimes," Andrew admitted. "Although my practice gave me the flexibility to also be involved in the family business."

They both turned at the sound of a door opening.

"What kind of business is that?" Cole asked as his gaze focused down the main hallway.

"O'Shea Sports." Andrew couldn't recall the last time he'd had to explain about the business. Back in Boston, the O'Shea family was well-known.

"No way." Cole might have said more, likely would have said more, but at that moment the women stepped into view.

Women, as in Sylvie and two friends. One must have

been Cole's wife, Meg, if the hug and kiss he gave her was an indication. The public display of such affection was foreign, but unlike his parents, Andrew didn't find it distasteful or unseemly.

Meg was tall and willowy with a mass of auburn hair and a face sprinkled with freckles. Her wide mouth held humor, and her eyes had sparkled the instant she spotted her husband. Josie Campbell, the bride-to-be, watched Meg and Cole with an understanding expression on her face.

Sylvie's gaze had gone instantly to Andrew.

He smiled and she crossed the waiting room to him, Josie at her side.

"I take it your luncheon has concluded?" he asked, widening his smile to include Josie.

"I hadn't seen the clinic since it was complete." Josie answered before Sylvie had a chance to speak. "Meg offered to show us around."

"I was surprised to see the van outside." Though Sylvie didn't look overly happy to see him, he sensed she wasn't bothered by his presence.

Andrew supposed he should take that as a positive. After all, had he really expected her to move into his arms like Meg had done with Cole? "I was at Hill of Beans grabbing some lunch and Cole asked if I wanted a tour."

"What do you think?" The husky voice had Andrew glancing to his right. Meg Lassiter extended her hand and introductions were exchanged.

"It has everything a doctor needs." Andrew thought of the clinics in various church basements. "Back in Boston I helped out in what we called 'pop-up' clinics. We were lucky to have an exam table. Compared to those places, this is the Ritz."

"We'll have to discuss those clinics sometime in more detail. What other communities are doing to meet the needs of the working poor are of real interest to me and many others in Jackson Hole." Meg pushed a hand back through her thick, curly hair, and he saw in her eyes the same passion he'd seen in Sylvie's whenever she mentioned creating a special cake. "But I promised Josie and Sylvie a tour. I've got a therapy scheduled in an hour, so the clock is ticking."

"I can show them around, Meg," Cole offered.

Josie exchanged a glance with Sylvie.

"Fine with me," Sylvie said.

"Let me show you the therapy area, real quick." Meg grabbed Josie's hand. "There's even a space eventually for a massage table. Right now we just have a chair."

"It's a good start." Josie followed Meg down the hall.

Sylvie glanced around. "This place is really nice."

"Since you're pressed for time now," Andrew said, "perhaps we can all get together another time. I'd be happy to tell you all you want to know."

"Noah and I want to come, too," Josie said. "I'm interested."

Meg cocked her head, her gaze settling on Sylvie. "Book club is next Tuesday at my house. If we can get Sylvie to agree to come, that'd be a good time."

Andrew frowned. This conversation was jumping around so much, he was having difficulty keeping up. "Book club?"

"I'll explain later. Just put Tuesday night in your

calendar." Cole leaned over and brushed a kiss across his wife's lips. "See you soon."

Meg gave him a wink, told her friends goodbye and sauntered off.

After the tour, Josie ended up taking Cole back downtown while Sylvie climbed into the van with Andrew.

Sylvie waited to speak until he'd wheeled the van in the direction of Spring Gulch and the house that Andrew was beginning to think of as home. "That's a nice setup they have there."

"State-of-the-art equipment." Andrew cast a sideways glance. "This is really a progressive community. I see why you like it here."

She relaxed back against the worn seat back. "It feels like home."

"Tell me what home was like for you."

She shot him a puzzled look, waved a dismissive hand. "I've told you all that before."

That was only partially the truth. Sylvie had told him the area of south Boston where she'd lived until fourth grade. She'd told him her father left when she was four and her mother took off when she was thirteen. He knew she'd found herself in foster care until she aged out. He'd tried to get her to tell him more about those times, but when she deflected the questions, he'd respected what he saw as her need for privacy.

Now Andrew wondered if that concern for her privacy had been a cop-out. It had hurt to think of the life she'd once led. Perhaps he didn't want to be reminded of it. The problem was, to know her, he needed to know her secrets.

"Tell me about what you remember when your father

left." It was only the first of many questions he planned
to ask. Discovering what made her tick was what this
trip was all about. And Andrew wasn't leaving until he
knew all of Sylvie's secrets.

Chapter Twelve

Sylvie wished she'd insisted Josie drive her home. But even as the thought crossed her mind she realized this might be the perfect opportunity. After she shared more about her background, if Andrew couldn't see just how unsuitable they were for each other, well, then he didn't want to see.

But she didn't want to share those painful memories in the car. Neither did she want to do it over dinner or pretending to relax with a glass of wine. "Stop the car."

He didn't quite slam on the brakes, but she did jerk forward in her seat as he wheeled the van to the side of the road and shifted into Park. "What's wrong?"

The worry in his eyes matched the concern in his voice. His gaze anxiously searched hers.

"I'm fine." The way her heart raced at his intense scrutiny made it a less-than-honest response, but she wanted to reassure him. "I want to walk."

Andrew sat back, stared at her as if she'd lost her mind. "You want to *walk* home?"

"No." Sylvie gave a little laugh, which sounded strained even to her own ears. "I just want to…walk."

He glanced down the busy ribbon of concrete. "Along the highway?"

"Hardly." She gave a halfhearted chuckle. "If we walk on the roadside, everyone will think the van broke down and want to give us a ride."

"If you say so." The puzzlement remained on his face. "If not down the road, where is it exactly you want to walk?"

She gestured off to the right, to a relatively flat span of ground made up primarily of dirt and scrubby plants. The mountains loomed far in the distance.

She saw his gaze drop to her shoes. Okay, they weren't hiking boots, but they were flat and comfortable. "I need to get out and move."

His gaze searched her and he shrugged. "Lead the way."

After a couple of minutes, Sylvie stumbled across a dirt trail of sorts winding its way through the brush. She wasn't sure what to think when Andrew took her hand but found the support steadied her.

"Any memories of my parents together were of them fighting." She kept her gaze focused straight ahead. "When he left, things were…quieter."

His fingers tightened around hers, but Andrew remained silent.

"It took me a while—quite a while, in fact—to realize that the man with the red hair who sometimes lifted me high in his arms to touch the ceiling was never coming back." She lifted one shoulder and let it fall.

"Though there was no more loud arguments, my mother was so angry. She bad-mouthed him all the time."

They walked for a couple of minutes in silence.

"What was hardest…" Sylvie paused and swallowed hard against the lump that had formed in her throat. "…was when she told me it made her sick to look at me."

Out of the corner of her eye, Sylvie saw Andrew's jaw clench. "Because you were his child?"

"That was probably part of it," Sylvie admitted. "I also looked like him. My hair wasn't as red as his, but our facial features… Well, it was easy to tell I was his daughter."

"The sins of the father…" he murmured.

"Exactly." Sylvie heaved a sigh. "For the next five years, I heard more times than I could count that my father was a coward who didn't even have the guts to tell her to her face he was leaving."

"Then she did the same thing to you nine years later."

"She did," Sylvie confirmed in a matter-of-fact tone as she climbed a small incline, Andrew still beside her. She tried not to think that she'd done virtually the same thing to Andrew three months ago.

"Tell me about when she left." Though uttered in a conversational tone, it was more of a demand than a request.

Thinking back to that horrible day, Sylvie felt her heart twist, but for only a moment. She reminded herself it had been a long, long time ago. She'd moved past the hurt and anger that had permeated her life for so many years of her childhood.

Once again Andrew appeared content to wait.

Sylvie paused at the top of a mound of dirt too small

to be called a hill. For a second she closed her eyes and inhaled deeply. She loved the scent of pine. "I came home from school and she wasn't there. That wasn't all that unusual. But the apartment appeared less...cluttered. It took me a while to realize that was because her stuff was gone."

"She'd moved out." His voice was soft, dangerously so.

"Yes." It was amazing to Sylvie that she could still choke up over something that had happened so many years ago.

"What did you do?"

"I waited for her to come back." A humorless smile lifted Sylvie's lips. "I may have only been an eighth grader, but I was pretty good at taking care of myself. Even when my mother was around, she'd get involved with the latest boyfriend and I'd be on my own until that relationship fell apart."

Andrew cursed under his breath.

"I made myself peanut butter sandwiches for dinner. There wasn't much food in the apartment, but if I was careful, I could make it last. Look." She pointed off in the distance where several deer grazed. "I suppose it's silly, but seeing wildlife up close still gives me a thrill."

His gaze settled on the animals. "It is pretty cool."

They remained where they stood for a few seconds, until the deer, obviously having caught their scent, bounded off toward the mountains.

"How long did you manage on your own?" he asked in the same conversational tone as she once again began to walk.

"Nearly two weeks." She couldn't keep the pride from her voice. "I washed my own clothes, made the meals—again, mostly peanut butter sandwiches—and got myself ready for school each morning."

"That's amazing."

The admiration in his tone made her smile, though what she'd done had been simple survival, certainly not anything praiseworthy.

"I did what I had to do." Her tone was matter-of-fact. "Any other kid in that situation would have done the same thing."

"I doubt that," he said. "You must have been frightened."

"Mostly at night," Sylvie admitted. "We didn't live in a great neighborhood and the apartment building… Well, let's just say many of the residents weren't pillars of the community."

"Who discovered your mother had left?"

"The landlord. He stopped by, demanding the rent. I got rid of him several times by telling him my mother wasn't at home, but that only worked for a couple of days. The man was a real bulldog." She gazed off into the distance, wondered if the chill she'd feel if she stepped onto those snowcapped slopes would equal the chill that had her now shivering in the bright sunshine. "They looked for her and eventually found her, but she told them she'd 'moved on.' I spent the next five years in a variety of foster homes, some good, others not so great. That's the story. Aren't you glad you asked?"

Sylvie didn't look at Andrew, didn't want to see the pity she knew she'd find in his eyes.

"That's quite a story."

"There are many who have it worse."

"You're a strong woman, Sylvie Thorne." The admiration, however misguided, warmed away some of the chill.

"I'm sorry I didn't speak with you before I left." The apology was spoken so softly that she wondered if he'd even hear. She'd cleared her throat, ready to repeat the words, when he spoke.

"I was surprised."

Three simple words that said so much by what they didn't say. *I expected better of you.*

"I still believe leaving was best, but—" she gave a bitter-sounding laugh "—that's probably what my mom and dad thought when they walked out on me. I handled it poorly. You deserved better."

"We both deserved better."

She nodded, the tightness in her chest making speech difficult at that moment.

"You obviously didn't know me well enough, didn't trust me enough, to feel as if you could share whatever concerns you had with me." His gaze searched hers. "There's still more you're not telling me. Like the reason you picked that night to walk."

While Sylvie wanted to be completely honest, what would be the point in bringing up the conversation with his father? No point, she told herself. "I—"

Andrew pressed a finger against her lips. "No lies."

She stiffened.

"Let me say simply that I hope when I'm ready to leave, you'll trust me enough, you'll have enough respect for what we've shared, to tell me everything." The smile that lifted his lips didn't reach his eyes. "If that happens, I'll consider this trip a success."

* * *

"Tell me again about this event." Andrew held open the car door for Sylvie, despite the fact that he knew she didn't expect it.

She slipped into the car he'd rented, a new SUV with leather seats and a moonroof that she was going to request he open on their drive into Jackson.

"What do you want to know?" She waited to speak until he was behind the wheel and the garage door had silently lifted.

"The name Jackson Hole Fall Arts Festival tells me some of what to expect, but not all."

"You want the entire scoop," she said with an easy smile tossed in his direction, "not just a spoonful of information."

"Exactly." Andrew wasn't sure why she appeared so relaxed, but he was grateful.

After their conversation this afternoon, a part of him had expected her to pull back. Instead she seemed more relaxed than she'd been since he first arrived. It was as if some kind of weight had been lifted from her shoulders.

The story she'd relayed troubled him, made him want to hit something, and he wasn't a violent guy. The thought of leaving a little girl alone…

"My sister's daughter, Anne Elizabeth, is nine," he heard himself say.

If Sylvie was surprised by the abrupt change in topic, it didn't show. "I never met her."

"Corinne and her family had been living in London. They'd only been back in the States for a couple of weeks before I left to come here."

"She was doing something with your European division, right?"

Sylvie had obviously listened the times he'd discussed O'Shea Sports.

"Corinne runs the company's European division." Andrew pulled into a space nearly a mile from the downtown area. Though he didn't know everything involved in this arts festival, he'd heard enough to know that the Palates and Palettes Gallery Walk going on this evening was very popular and he was unlikely to find a closer spot. "She's a dynamo."

"Is she back to visit?" Sylvie met him on the sidewalk as he rounded the front of the SUV.

"For now. She and her husband want to move back to the States." Andrew took Sylvie's arm as they started down the sidewalk toward the downtown district. It was automatic. While he'd never been into handholding before, in the time that he and Sylvie had been together it had become second nature. "She'd like to be the next COO of O'Shea Sports. She came to try to convince my father to change his mind."

"Change his mind?"

"I'm assuming the position as of October 1."

Sylvie stopped, just stopped in the center of the sidewalk, her face a study in confusion. "I knew your father was hoping to convince you to take that job, but you already have one. You're a doctor."

"My father is adamant that an O'Shea male succeeds him." Andrew made no excuses for his father's antiquated ideas. God knew, he'd tried his best to get his dad to change his mind on this matter.

"Do you want to do it?"

"It's expected."

"That isn't what I asked."

"I owe it to my father, to the family." Andrew pressed his lips together. If not for him, Thomas would be at the helm and everyone would be happy.

As he'd expected, the traffic on the sidewalk began to increase exponentially the closer they came to the downtown shopping area.

"I'd say I can't believe we never talked about this." Sylvie's lips quirked up in a wry smile. "Except we didn't do a lot of talking back in Boston."

"It wasn't all about sex," he said, a bit indignant over the accusation.

"I'm not blaming you." Her eyes sparkled. "I was as hot to hop into the sack as you were."

An older woman with silver-gray hair and a black cane with a shiny silver handle turned an assessing gaze in their direction. After only a second she smiled and turned back to her companion, an older gentleman with a neatly trimmed goatee wearing a beret.

"Back to the topic at hand." Sylvie slowed her steps to put some distance between them and the older couple. "Was taking over the company always in your plans?"

This would be the time to bring up Thomas. Andrew had always felt guilty for not speaking more of his brother. Though what had happened wasn't a secret, the accident wasn't something often brought up in his family. It was just too painful.

Andrew didn't want to go back down that road, not tonight. The evening was off to a good start. And Sylvie was in an upbeat mood. Later, they could discuss it.

"Is that one of the galleries we should check out?" Andrew gestured with one hand, hoping she'd let it go for now. "Judging by all the people streaming inside, it appears to be a popular place."

"It's very popular." Sylvie pulled a brochure from her purse. She read for a second, then glanced back at him. "They're featuring the works of a big-time Montana wildlife painter."

Andrew couldn't help it—his lips twitched. He rubbed his chin as they stopped and stepped to the side. "Big-time, eh? Is that what it says in the brochure?"

She swatted him with the rolled-up piece of paper. For a second it was as if the past three months away from each other had never been. "If you want the exact words, Mr. High Society, I'll read them to you."

Somehow Andrew managed to keep a straight face. "I'd appreciate that courtesy."

Sylvie rolled her eyes and began to read. "'Presenting new works by acclaimed Montana wildlife artist Kyle Sims.'"

Andrew experienced a flash of recognition. "I know his works. Or rather of them. The artist is well-known for the natural realism of his works. One of my father's friends owns several paintings."

"Well, then you should enjoy the show. It says these are new studio paintings."

When they walked into the large gallery, Andrew realized somehow her hand was back in his. He tucked it through his arm, drawing her even closer to him as they began to stroll.

The air seemed to buzz with electricity, or maybe it was that familiar charge that hit him whenever Sylvie was close. Just as it was difficult to tell if the intoxicating floral scent came from her shampoo or from the cylindrical silver urns filled with towering gladioli, hydrangeas and palms placed strategically around the gallery.

A waiter dressed in black tie, holding a tray of champagne flutes, paused to ask if they'd like a glass.

Andrew lifted two glasses from the tray and handed one to Sylvie.

"Trying to get me drunk?" Sylvie teased, raising the glass to her lips.

"I'd prefer you be fully conscious for what I have in mind for later," he shot back, enjoying the easy repartee.

It had been like this from the beginning, Andrew realized, an easy give-and-take coupled with lighthearted teasing always underscored by a punch of lust.

They moved to inspect a painting that depicted a red fox standing on a rock formation looking over his shoulder.

"I love this." Sylvie's eyes widened with admiration. "It's so real I feel as if I'm there. It's like he's taunting me, saying, 'Are you going to follow me or not?'"

Andrew could tell her admiration was sincere. "You really like it?"

She nodded. "Don't you?"

He simply nodded and then put his palm against the small of her back and guided her to the next painting. By the time they'd made it through the gallery, Sylvie had found plenty of paintings she liked but none as much as the red fox.

"Would you mind waiting for me while I check out the restroom?"

Andrew smiled. "I can amuse myself."

While she was away, he strode over to one of the gallery employees and conducted some business. Once that was concluded, he followed up on several of his clients back in Boston. While he felt confident in the ability of the doctor he'd left in charge, these were his patients and one of them, Mrs. Whitaker, had been struggling with some recent health setbacks.

He'd just pocketed his phone when he saw Sylvie crossing the gallery floor. For tonight's event, she wore a simple skirt and top in a blue that made her eyes look like violets. Though he'd always liked her hair with its riot of curls, this new sleek version was also attractive.

Judging from the admiring glances sent her way, he wasn't the only man who'd noticed.

Mine.

The thought came swift and hard. Though it wouldn't be that way forever, for now, for as long as he remained in Jackson Hole, they were a couple.

Andrew didn't wait for her to come to him. He crossed the room with long strides. When he reached her, he pulled her into his arms and kissed her.

Not the kind of kiss a friend would give a friend, but one a man would give a woman he desired.

"What was that for?" Sylvie's laugh was breathless as the kiss ended and she stepped back.

"Consider it—" he couldn't stop the quick flash of a grin "—an appetizer."

Chapter Thirteen

An appetizer?

Sylvie didn't press Andrew for an explanation. The thought of what might be on the agenda when they got home had her heart doing flip-flops the entire way back to Spring Gulch. She kept the conversation light. It had been a wonderful day and she knew much of the reason had to do with being with Andrew.

Though she knew she'd be heartbroken when he left Jackson Hole, she'd made the decision when she walked out of that gallery tonight that she was going to enjoy these next few weeks. And if he left, *when* he left, she would hold the memories of these days together tight to her heart.

"I'm surprised you weren't asked to do any of the desserts featured at various galleries tonight." There was more than a hint of righteous indignation in his tone. "Yours are every bit as good as the ones we sampled."

Sylvie slipped off her shoes and sank into the soft buttery leather of the living room sofa, wiggling her toes.

Andrew turned once flames danced cheerily in the hearth. Though the temperature outside was a balmy forty-five degrees, he'd insisted on starting a fire.

Sylvie hadn't argued. It wasn't her home. Besides, she rather liked having a fire.

Without asking permission, Andrew dropped down beside her, lifting his arm to rest around her shoulders.

What the heck? Sylvie thought and rested her head comfortably against his shoulder.

"I could get us some wine," he said, making no move to get up.

"I'm fine." She breathed in the scent of him that had once been so familiar, so dear, then found herself blinking back unexpected tears.

"Why didn't even one place have your cakes?" Andrew pressed. "If this event is supposed to showcase the best Jackson Hole has in terms of art and wine and fine cuisine, you should have been featured."

The irritation had returned to his voice. Sylvie had no doubt that if this was his community and he was familiar with the event organizers, he'd have had them on the phone right now.

"I'll be involved in Taste of the Tetons on Sunday," she told him, stroking his arm with her hand, simply because she felt the need to touch. "I didn't move here in time to line up contracts to provide hors d'oeuvres for tonight's festivities."

Andrew took a moment and appeared to consider

her explanation. "Some of those other cakes were nice," he said finally, "but none were in your league, not in taste or in creativity."

"You like my designs?" Sylvie couldn't keep the surprise from her voice. For some reason, she'd gotten the impression back in Boston that he found her designs a bit too avant-garde for his tastes.

"Absolutely." His eyebrows drew together. "Did you think I didn't?"

"I wasn't sure," she said honestly. "My work isn't exactly mainstream."

"I'm a very nontraditional guy."

Sylvie snorted. She couldn't help it. She didn't know anyone *more* mainstream than Andrew Dalton O'Shea.

"I'm not," he decreed in an imperious manner. "Unlike many of my friends, I'm open to new ideas and new experiences."

Sylvie raised a skeptical eyebrow. "Seriously? You expect me to believe that?"

"It's the truth."

"It's not the truth." Sylvie didn't intend to be mean, but she couldn't let Andrew spout such falsehoods without challenging the assertions. "You live in your own little world, a world composed of symphonies and operas and polo matches."

"I knew I'd regret showing you my polo mounts."

"Your polo ponies were very sweet and quite pretty."

Andrew winced. "I didn't purchase them because they were pretty. I got them because not only did they exhibit speed and stamina, but they showed good balance and an unexcitable temperament."

"I still think they're pretty."

Andrew cocked his head as a thought occurred to him. "Have you ever ridden a horse?"

"Me?" Amusement bubbled up inside Sylvie. "The closest I came to riding was being hauled around Central Park in one of those carriages when I was in culinary school."

"I'll teach you to ride."

For a second she thought he was joking, but those beautiful gray eyes were serious.

"You're not going to be here that long."

"We'll fit it in."

"Don't make promises you can't keep." Though Sylvie kept her tone light, she meant every word. "It's enough that we've agreed to spend these next three weeks together."

His chin lifted in that rarely seen stubborn tilt. "I *am* going to teach you to ride."

"If it works out, that'd be wonderful," Sylvie conceded, but wasn't holding her breath. She'd learned long ago not to count on promises. Even ones made with the best of intentions.

"You don't trust me."

She blinked. "Where did that come from?"

"You don't trust that I'll take you riding, even though I said I would."

"I just know that these next few weeks are going to be very bus—"

"You didn't believe I liked your work, even though I always told you how much I liked and admired what you do."

She waved an airy hand. "We were sleeping together. What else were you going to say?"

His only reply was a stony stare.

Realizing this was getting awkward, Sylvie sought to defuse the situation. "C'mon, Andrew. Don't make a big deal out of nothing."

"It's not nothing." His jaw lifted in a stubborn tilt. "You don't trust that what I say is true, even though I've given you no reason to distrust me."

"People disappoint," she blurted out. "People lie. They say what you want to hear. My foster parents were always telling me that my mother loved me. But she didn't. You don't run away from someone you love. You don't leave them alone."

"You ran away from me," he said, his gaze never leaving hers. "Does that mean you didn't love me?"

"You weren't alone. You have your family. They love you and you love them." She clamped her lips together, realizing she'd only made the situation worse in trying to explain.

"Sometimes, Sylvie, you have to trust. Or you're never going to be close to anybody."

After another thirty minutes of civilized conversation, Sylvie went off to bed. Andrew knew he'd never be able to sleep, so he added another log to the fire, poured himself a glass of wine and retrieved his laptop.

The house was quiet when he settled himself on the sofa in front of the fire with his laptop. As he read through his messages, he admitted leaving his patients had been more difficult than he thought. While he knew his associate had been taking good care of them, he was the one who knew them and their medical history inside and out.

Like eighty-nine-year-old Fern Whitaker. He'd been her physician ever since he began his concierge practice. Her husband had died twenty years ago. Her children were all in other states and she now lived alone in the grand home on Beacon Hill where she and her husband had raised those five children.

The children worried she was depressed, but he knew much of what ailed her was loneliness. Especially during the long winter months. She wasn't a complainer. When she told him during one of his weekly visits that she'd been short of breath lately, he'd taken the complaint seriously.

Right before he left Boston, he'd diagnosed her with a pulmonary embolism. The blood clot in her lung had been a large one. Since she'd experienced problems on anticoagulants before, Andrew had hooked her up with a top-notch surgeon who'd removed the clot during a surgery.

His associate, Dr. Seth Carstairs, had been keeping Andrew updated on her recovery, but it wasn't the same as being there.

Andrew frowned at the email from Seth. Fern had been refusing to wear the compression stockings ordered post-surgery. He wondered what was going on. Normally Fern was compliant with medical orders. He shot off a quick email to Seth, asking him to call tomorrow with details.

There were several emails from his father, updating him on recent activities of the company. While Andrew had worked for O'Shea Sports during college, the business world had never held much interest.

Still, he forced himself through the attached reports and graphs before shifting to an email from his sister.

Hers contained business news, too, as well as family updates. If only their father could see that Corinne was the perfect person to take the company to new heights in the twenty-first century.

The rest of the emails he skimmed, then set aside the laptop, leaned back against the plush leather and sipped his wine.

The evening, prior to the return home, had gone better than he'd anticipated. In fact, he'd had high hopes that the night would end with her sharing his bed. Instead all the talking they'd been doing had yielded an unexpected result.

She didn't trust him. In fact, had never trusted him.

The realization was like a knife to the heart. He'd never given her any reason to distrust his word or his feelings for her, yet there was no denying the fact.

He was almost positive that the distrust was part of the reason she left. Despite the ring on her finger, the promises they'd made to each other, she hadn't trusted he loved her. Likely she thought he'd get tired of her and move on. Just as her mother and father had done all those years ago.

There was probably more to her leaving than that, although this lack of trust seemed more than enough reason. When he found himself attempting to figure out a way to build that trust, he reined in the impulse by reminding himself that he'd come to Jackson Hole to get to know Sylvie. The purpose in getting to know her was so he could accept he hadn't known the woman he thought he loved.

That fact had been shoved in his face tonight. He should be able to go home knowing she'd never trusted him.

But knowing wasn't enough to give him peace. He needed more. And he would get more. From where he sat, there was still a lot for him to know about Sylvie Thorne.

Though sorely tempted to tell Sylvie he was going to sleep in, Andrew dragged himself up and went with her to the bakery, then rode with her while they delivered baked goods to all of her clients.

"Instead of hanging around here, I'm going to the health clinic and see how the grand opening is going. If they're swamped I may stick around and lend a hand." Andrew kept his tone polite.

They'd been very polite all morning.

"That's fine." Sylvie pulled the van into its parking spot. "I have a lot of prep work to do before tomorrow."

He must have looked blank, because she smiled. "The Taste of the Tetons."

"That's right." For some reason he'd forgotten all about the open-air tasting fair on Sunday. "Text when you get done and we can find a time to meet."

The smile she flashed him didn't quite reach her eyes. "Sounds like a plan."

Andrew got in his car, but instead of heading to the clinic, he stopped by the gallery and picked up his purchase. Only after safely storing it in the spare bedroom at home did he turn the car in the direction of the clinic.

As the parking lot was full, he was forced to find a space down the road. He discovered part of the reason for the congested lot was Cole's coffee cart and a bouncy house for kids.

If the purpose of the grand opening was to draw out the citizens of Jackson Hole, it appeared the efforts had been a success. Even as Andrew strolled to the beverage cart, the physician in him wondered how things were progressing on the inside.

Before he got close to the cart, Keenan appeared out of the crowd. "Mitzi will be happy to see you."

Immediately Andrew went on alert. "What's the problem?"

"Too many patients." Keenan flashed a grin. "Too few doctors. Did you mean what you said about wanting to help?"

"Absolutely." Even as he spoke, Andrew turned toward the front door.

"Not that way." Keenan steered him around back to an unmarked door. He unlocked it and motioned Andrew inside.

The entrance opened into the back office area.

Andrew stepped into a beehive, a well-organized beehive to be sure, but one alive with activity. Doctors in lab coats and nurses in brightly colored uniforms wove in and out of exam and treatment rooms with quick steps.

"Dr. McGregor," Keenan called out to his wife when she stepped from a room. "Look what I brought you. Fresh meat and he's ready and willing to help."

"I owe you." Her gaze locked with her husband's.

"I'll figure out a way you can repay me." The suggestive edge to his voice wasn't lost on any of them.

"Looking forward to it." She turned to Andrew. "I really appreciate this. We knew it would be busy and thought we were staffed for it, but we've been slammed ever since the doors opened."

"Put me where you need me." Andrew experienced a surge of excitement. He hadn't even been gone from medicine a week and he was already champing at the bit.

"Room five." Mitzi gestured to a pretty redheaded nurse. "Leila will be the RN assisting you. You'll find a clean lab coat in the closet in the room."

With Leila at his side, Andrew was off to the races. The afternoon flew by. Each time an exam room emptied out, the competent RN retrieved another patient from the overcrowded waiting room. He found himself enjoying the variety of ages and conditions.

He treated everyone from a four-year-old with foot and mouth disease to an octogenarian with a sprained ankle. Though there wasn't much time for conversation, Andrew gave each patient his full attention.

By the time the doors were closed, he was tired but surprisingly energized.

Mitzi placed a hand on his shoulder. "Thank you again. We couldn't have done it without you."

"It was my pleasure."

Her gaze searched his face. "I believe you mean it."

"I do." His tone was unapologetic. "Some people love to draw or paint or write. Or bake, like Sylvie. From the time I was small, I liked taking something broken and making it whole."

"That's sweet."

Andrew turned and found Sylvie standing there. "Did you get all your prep done?"

"I did." She turned toward Mitzi. "Appears the grand opening was a huge success."

"Extremely well received. And this guy—" Mitzi patted his shoulder "—was a lifesaver."

"She exaggerates," Andrew told Sylvie.

"I'm not exaggerating and I do owe you." Mitzi paused. "Do you and Sylvie have plans for dinner?"

You and Sylvie. After only a week, they were already being seen as a couple.

Andrew exchanged a glance with Sylvie. She shrugged.

"Keenan and I are going to Perfect Pizza once we get out of here," Mitzi said. "We'd love to have you join us."

"Pizza sounds good to me." Andrew glanced at Sylvie. After last night, he wasn't sure what she wanted.

Sylvie's gaze shifted to Keenan when he walked up. "Your wife invited us to join you for pizza. But I don't want to crash your romantic evening."

"That's later." Keenan flashed a grin. "Pizza first. Romance later."

When Mitzi rolled her shoulders, Keenan stepped close and began to rub.

"How about we meet you at the restaurant in thirty minutes?" Mitzi closed her eyes and moaned in pleasure when her husband found a knot.

"We can take my car," Andrew said casually to Sylvie. "No need trying to find two parking spots downtown."

On the way downtown she told him all about the preparation she'd done for tomorrow's event.

"It sounds like it's big."

"I haven't been here for one," she said as he pulled onto the highway leading into Jackson, "but these kinds of events seem to draw in both the locals and the tourists."

"How does it work, this Taste of Jackson Hole?"

"Taste of the Tetons," she corrected. "From what I understand, each taste ticket costs you a buck. In this huge open-air tasting area, there will be alley chefs, restaurants and caterers putting their culinary work on display for sampling."

"Let me get this straight." Andrew felt himself relaxing as they continued to chat amiably. "I buy a ticket for a dollar and I can taste one of your little cakes?"

"That's basically it, but not quite." Sylvie shifted slightly in her seat to angle toward him. "Again, from what I've been told, tastes range from two to four tickets."

"That makes sense." Andrew felt a surge of triumph when he snagged a parking spot only a couple of blocks from Perfect Pizza. When he shut off the engine, he turned to Sylvie. "Have you ever eaten at this place?"

She shook her head. "I've heard it's really good pizza."

"Mitzi and Keenan must think so."

"This will be another first."

Andrew puzzled over the comment on their walk to the restaurant. Later, on their way home after an enjoyable dinner, he finally realized what Sylvie had meant.

They'd never gone out with another couple when they were together in Boston. He had several friends who were married he could have called up and made arrangements for the four of them to go out. Likewise, Sylvie had several friends from the bakery where she worked who were in relationships. But she'd never suggested they get together.

The reasons didn't matter now. What mattered was that he was getting to know her here, in a way that perhaps had not been possible in Boston.

What he was realizing was that the more he got to know, the more he wanted to know. Which meant he wasn't going anywhere, at least not anytime soon.

Chapter Fourteen

As was quickly becoming their custom, if you could
count a couple of days in a row a custom, once Andrew
and Sylvie returned home they gravitated to the great
room. Andrew built a fire while Sylvie poured them each
a glass of wine.

Though they needed to get up early, it was only eight
o'clock and Sylvie was too wired by the cola she'd drunk
with her pizza to even think about sleep.

"Did you really used to put splints on birds when
you were a boy?" she asked once they'd exhausted the
clinic and pizza subjects.

His lips quirked up. "Splints on birds, dressings on
cats and dogs. If I could have gotten my parents to
agree, I'd have treated my family's injuries."

Sylvie chuckled and took a sip of wine. "It sounds
as if your passion became apparent from an early age."

"My favorite gift when I was five was a doctor set."

"I don't think I got any gifts that year." Sylvie thought back to that year after her dad had left and shook her head. "No. Once my dad left, money was pretty tight."

Not wanting to spend even one more second discussing those times in her life, Sylvie turned the subject back to Andrew. "I hope you plan on continuing your practice even after you take over that position at O'Shea Sports."

The silence that cast a pall over the room gave her the answer even before he spoke.

"I'd like to continue to practice medicine," he said slowly, "but being COO is a huge commitment of both time and energy. I don't know that there'll be any of me left over for medicine."

Something told her he was expecting her to argue the point, to insist that if you wanted something enough you made time for it. Sylvie knew that wasn't always true, just as he did.

"When I lived in Boston, I had to work to pay my bills. I'd received some grants to attend school, but I'd also had to take out some loans. I wanted to be free of them, so for two years before I met you, I made that my mission." She brought the glass of wine to her lips but didn't take a drink. "I worked both as a waitress and at the bakery. I had some opportunities at the bakery to be creative, but only within their specified—and rather rigid—parameters."

"I suppose you're going to tell me that you still found time for your own creations."

"No." Her gaze met his. "By the time I got home from my waitress job, I was exhausted. I'd fall into bed, then had to be at the bakery at four a.m. for my shift. If any free time existed, I was too tired to search for it."

Andrew's eyebrows drew together in puzzlement. "I don't recall you working at a restaurant."

"Two months before I met you, I paid off the last of my student loans. I gave my notice at L'Espalier the next day." She didn't even try to fight the pride that welled up inside her. Paying off those loans had been a huge accomplishment.

"I'm impressed." The admiration in his eyes made her squirm.

"I didn't tell you to toot my own horn. I just wanted to say that I believe you're right. Once you take that position with O'Shea Sports, the practice of medicine may indeed be relegated to your past." The thought of anyone having to give up their passion saddened her, but when that person was Andrew… She gazed into the fire. "It was difficult to give up creating my own cakes. Still, I knew within two years I'd be back doing it again. If I'd had to give it up entirely… I don't know what would have happened to me, to the *essence* of me."

Andrew spoke slowly and deliberately. "I don't believe I ever realized before now just how much your creative design meant to you. I know I didn't give it the consideration it deserved when we talked about how melding our lives together would look."

Sylvie couldn't dispute what he said. But neither would she let him take all the blame. "Growing up as I did, I got used to people telling me what to do. I wanted to make you happy. I thought by going along with whatever you wanted, I would be content. I don't think that would have been the case. I've come to believe that to make someone else happy, you have to be comfortable in your own skin."

"You seem content in your own skin now."

"I am," she agreed, "and so are you. For now."

He gave her a curious look.

"You're happy now, but once you take that COO position, you won't be. You're a doctor, Andrew. Healing people is what you were put on this earth to do."

He downed the rest of his wine and surged to his feet. "It's been a long day. You and I have to be up and rolling out of here in less than six hours."

Which meant, she decided, that the conversation had come to an end. Sylvie took the hand he offered and rose to her feet.

Even after she stood, her hand remained clasped in his.

"You've given me a lot to think about," he said, then lowered his lips to hers.

The kiss might have been short and sweet, but it sent a pleasurable tingle all the way to the tips of her toes.

"Good night, Sylvie."

"Good night," she called out, but he didn't turn as he strode from the room.

The urge to follow him into his bedroom was nearly overwhelming. Sylvie moved to the window on the far side of the room and pressed her forehead against the cold glass.

Something was happening between them. She only wished she knew what in the heck to do about it.

Andrew wanted to help Sylvie work her station at the Taste of the Tetons, but long before he'd arrived in Jackson Hole, she'd enlisted several of her friends to assist with the event that ran from 11:00 until 4:00 p.m. They'd helped her carry in her goodies, which included cupcakes that looked as if the Wicked Witch was buried in the frosting to ones that resembled beautiful flowers. There were bouquets of "cake pops," and for the more traditionally minded, there were tiny desserts that looked so much like flowers he couldn't tell them from the real thing.

Though it appeared he wasn't needed, Andrew was reluctant to leave. "Are you sure there isn't anything I can do to help?"

He saw Josie glance curiously in his direction before she returned her attention to arranging the Wicked Witches on a cupcake tower made to resemble a winding yellow brick road.

"Thanks for the offer." Sylvie looked up and smiled. With a true artist's eye, she'd interspersed the lavender and white hydrangea cupcakes on an elegant tower where real flowers and greenery were strategically interspersed. "But we've got this under control."

On the other side of her, Poppy kept moving one of several elegant "cake pop bouquets" around, looking for the perfect spot on the linen-clad table.

Of all the items on display, however, Andrew's favorite was the couture cupcake stand of the upper body of a mannequin in a sleeveless black dress, surrounded by mini cups filled with cake pieces and chocolate mousse.

The display, including the clothesline across the front of the booth, with tiny clothespins holding her brightly colored handmade business cards, drew Andrew's eye. He plucked a card off the line and dropped it into his pocket.

"I'll be back at four to help clean up."

Sylvie looked up and smiled. "That'd be great. Have a good afternoon."

Seeing no choice, Andrew walked away. It wasn't as if he wasn't capable of amusing himself. But amusing himself wasn't the issue. He wanted to share this day with Sylvie, wanted to stroll down the aisles and consider the food options. But he reminded himself she had work to do. He respected that fact…and her talent.

Because he knew if he stayed in the Taste of the Tetons tent, he'd have eventually wound his way back to Sylvie's booth, he stepped out and over to one holding the Wine Tasting and Silent Auction.

He was sampling a particularly fine Syrah when he was punched in the shoulder. "Hey, Boston, what's that you're drinkin'?"

Andrew recognized Keenan's voice even before he turned. Even though the day was in the midsixties, the man looked ready for a lumberjack festival in a flannel shirt, jeans and boots.

"Syrah." Andrew lifted his glass holding a red so dark you couldn't even see through it.

Keenan lifted the glass from his hand and took a swig. A thoughtful expression crossed his face. "Tastes like smoked meat. I like it."

With that pronouncement, he downed the rest of the contents and then handed Andrew the empty glass.

"It's particularly good for you because it has a high level of tannins." Andrew set the glass down on a nearby tray. "Lots of health-benefiting antioxidants."

"It tastes like smoked meat."

Andrew grinned. "That, too."

"Mitzi is working the clinic today," Keenan told him before he had a chance to ask.

"Sylvie's got a booth in the other tent."

Keenan's gaze sharpened. "You two seem to be seeing a lot of each other."

Realizing that when he left, Sylvie would be left to

deal with the speculation and questions, Andrew kept his reply simple. "We were friends back in Boston."

"If I had to speculate, I'd say you were more than friends." Keenan paused to order a bottle of the Syrah before turning back. "But I don't speculate."

Andrew found himself liking Keenan McGregor. Somehow, without a word being said, he and Keenan explored the tent together.

Once they'd tasted their share of wine, they wandered over to where local artists had set up. The sign indicated this was the 17th Annual Takin' It to the Streets Art Fair.

Keenan gestured to a picture of a large elk with piercing dark eyes. "That one reminds me of Mitzi when she's pissed at me."

Andrew chuckled. Sylvie had chosen wisely when she picked Jackson Hole. The community had so much to offer. No doubt she'd eventually find someone special and settle down. It was apparent she was happy here in a way she'd never been happy back in Boston, in a way that she'd never been happy with him.

The thought left a bitter taste in his mouth.

He'd tried to make her happy, had wanted to make her happy, but in the end they'd failed each other. As he and Keenan moved down the sidewalk filled with artists, Andrew realized that was the bitterest pill of all to swallow.

The Taste of the Tetons experience left Sylvie both exhausted and exhilarated. She'd made a lot of new connections and had given out a ton of business cards.

Because she'd been watching, she'd noticed how the eyes of potential clients lit up when she mentioned she'd recently worked with Kathy Randall on a Sweet Adelines event.

"I'm beginning to think Kathy was right," Sylvie said to Andrew that evening while she whipped together a grilled chicken and wheat-berry salad for dinner.

After indulging in too many sweets, they'd both been ready for something healthy.

"What was she right about?" he asked, putting napkins and silverware on the table, while the bottle of Grüner Veltliner he'd picked up at the wine auction breathed on the counter.

"She told me that the best way to get referrals is to become involved in the community." Sylvie shifted her attention to him while she tossed the salad. "I may have to join Sweet Adelines after all."

"Would that be so bad?"

"I've never been much of a joiner."

"It sounds like growing up you were never in any place long enough to join different clubs and activities."

"That's true," she concurred. "And most of that kind of stuff cost money I didn't have."

"Not to mention once you got out of culinary school, you were too busy working to make a living and pay off your loans to do anything extra." Andrew added ice and water to some square glass tumblers.

Sylvie thought about what he'd said, then nodded. "You're right. Just because I've never joined groups in the past doesn't mean I can't join now."

"And just because something didn't work in the past doesn't mean it won't work now." *Like us*, he thought, then shoved the notion aside. "Do you like to sing?"

She considered. "I enjoyed it the other night."

"You should give it a try."

"I think I will."

"Good."

They exchanged a smile as Andrew turned to pour the wine.

Andrew had no idea what to expect at the Tuesday night book-club meeting held at Cole and Meg's mountain home. Neither he nor Sylvie had been told what book would be discussed. He only knew the dress was casual, which seemed to be how most events were in Jackson Hole, and that they needed to bring only themselves.

"I feel naked," Sylvie whispered to him as they stepped into the great room filled with both adults and children.

"Really?" Andrew grinned. "Did you decide to go commando?"

Puzzlement blanketed her face, and then she rolled her eyes. "I am so used to bringing something. But Meg insisted everything was covered."

"That doesn't tell me if you're wearing underwear."

Her answer was an elbow jab to his side.

He grinned. Over the past few days, things between them had settled into a comfortable routine. Despite the fact that they hadn't slept together since he first arrived, Andrew felt closer to her than he had when they were sleeping together every night in Boston.

"Glad you could make it." Cole clapped a hand on his back and smiled at Sylvie.

"Thanks for inviting us." Sylvie glanced around, her eyes wide. "This must be one big book club."

Meg slipped through the crowd to give Sylvie a hug. "Actually, the book-club discussion is held in the kitchen after we eat. Females only. No males allowed."

"Thank God." Cole pretended to wipe sweat from his brow.

"There are a lot of men here," Sylvie observed. "What do they do?"

It was the question on the tip of Andrew's tongue. If Sylvie hadn't asked it, he would have. He also wondered about all the children in the room.

"After we eat, the men are relegated to the great room to do, well, whatever they want to do. The children go downstairs. Whoever hosts is responsible for hiring the babysitters." Meg's gaze shifted from Andrew to Sylvie. "Keep that in mind when it's your turn to host."

Andrew saw Sylvie open her mouth, obviously to inform their host and hostess that he wouldn't be around that long and she certainly didn't have the space. But he spoke first. "Good to know."

The ringing of a bell had them turning their heads.

"Time to eat." Meg slipped her arm through Sylvie's and led her toward the buffet tables.

"She needs this," Andrew murmured, almost to himself. "This connection. It matters."

"That's the great thing about Jackson Hole," Cole said. "It doesn't take long before you're considered family."

A family was something Sylvie had never experienced. If she'd stayed in Boston, he doubted she'd have found it there. His sister would have made her welcome, but Corinne didn't even live in the same country. His parents, while good people, weren't the warm and fuzzy kind.

He thought of the argument he'd had with his father the night before Sylvie left. The old man had practically threatened to disown him if he married Sylvie.

Though he knew his father wouldn't have gone to that extreme, Andrew had felt the need to make it clear his loyalties lay with Sylvie.

It was too bad Sylvie hadn't felt that same loyalty to him…

But the anger that had always surged whenever he thought of her leaving didn't come. Instead he was seized with a renewed determination to figure out just what had led her to leave him that particular night.

"I know you've been living in your friend's place in Spring Gulch," Cole said as they stood back and let the others swarm the food.

"It's a nice enough place."

"Are you thinking that's the area where you'd like to build?" Cole rocked back on his heels. "Or are you looking at the mountains?"

Andrew hesitated. While he'd made no secret of the fact that he liked Jackson Hole, he wondered where Cole could have gotten the idea he was considering moving here. Not only moving here, but building a home.

Even as he pondered the thought, his gaze settled on Sylvie. He smiled when he saw her laughing with Poppy Campbell and Meg.

He pulled his gaze back to Cole, who was sipping a Dos Equis straight from the bottle. "My home is in Boston."

"I grew up here," Cole said. "I got out as soon as I could and never planned to come back."

"Why did you?"

A shadow crossed Cole's face. "A couple that I was very close to were killed in a car accident. Meg and I, we weren't together at the time, were given joint custody of their son, Charlie. His parents specified he be raised here."

"Couldn't you have gotten around that stipulation?"

"Probably. But in the end that stipulation ended up being the best thing for Meg, for me and for Charlie." Cole took a long pull. "I've learned those crazy things often end up being unexpected blessings."

Andrew's thoughts went immediately to Sylvie. The way she'd left. The way he'd followed her here. The closeness that had developed between them.

Unexpected blessing?

Time, he decided, would tell that story.

Chapter Fifteen

By the time Sylvie and Andrew got home, it was nearly ten. Neither of them was ready for bed. Instead of having more wine, Sylvie decided to make some tea.

Andrew followed her into the kitchen, then leaned his back against the countertop and watched her. "Seriously? You didn't even discuss a book?"

"That's right." Though he remained fully dressed, Sylvie stood in bare feet while she brewed chamomile tea. Her lips curved up. "Mary Karen Fisher started talking about going skinny-dipping. Then everyone else started telling tales. *Moby Dick* was forgotten."

"*Moby Dick?*" He straightened. "That's the book you discussed?"

"That was the book we were *supposed* to discuss. I don't think we could have had a good discussion, because it didn't appear anyone in attendance had read it." Sylvie lifted the two mugs and carried them to the small dinette table.

Andrew pulled out her chair, then took a seat opposite her. "You had fun."

"I did." She took a sip of tea. "Did you enjoy yourself?"

The men had watched a replay of that week's Monday night football game. Cole had made sure to introduce him to Joel Dennes and Gabe Davis, who spoke with him about available lots in Jackson Hole.

Andrew still wondered why he hadn't just simply said he wasn't interested. Instead he'd told them that while he wasn't interested in a mountain lot because of the distance into Jackson, he'd be willing to consider something in Spring Gulch.

The crazy thing was, he hadn't been thinking of himself when he made that decision. He'd been thinking of Sylvie. The last thing he'd want was for her to be driving down those steep mountain roads at 3:00 a.m.

He pulled his eyebrows together. What had he been thinking? Even if he wanted to stay, he couldn't. He owed it to his family, to Tommy's memory, to take this position at O'Shea Sports.

The thought made him irritable.

"Something on your mind?" Her soft voice broke through his thoughts.

He jerked his head up. "What makes you think something is wrong?"

She smiled slightly. "I didn't ask if something is wrong. I asked if something was on your mind."

Her eyes were watchful as they studied him over the top of her mug.

"What made you leave?" The question burst from his lips with none of the finesse he'd envisioned.

"I told you—"

"I know what you said," he interrupted, not giving her a chance to continue. "But why that particular night? Why not before the party? Or several days later?"

"I—" She turned toward the window. "Look, it's starting to rain."

Andrew glanced at the window, noticing for the first time the water on the glass, hearing the sound on the roof. It distracted him, but for only a second.

"Why, Sylvie?" His voice was soft and low now, the same tone he often used to soothe frightened patients. "Was it something I said? Or did?"

She lowered her lids but not soon enough to shield her reaction. It had been something he'd said. But what could it have been? He searched his memories but came up empty.

"I can see in your eyes I was to blame."

"You weren't to blame." Her sudden vehemence had him pulling back, but her hand remained in his. "Don't ever think you were to blame."

"Tell me." He kept his voice soft, inviting confidences. "Please."

He wasn't sure if it was the *please* that did it or perhaps it was simply that the time had finally come for this truth to be revealed, but Sylvie expelled a shuddering breath.

When she attempted to pull her hand back, he kept hold, gently stroking her palm with his thumb.

"I'm not angry." Andrew's gaze remained focused on her face. "I simply want to understand."

She opened her mouth, then closed it.

He was just about to reassure her again when she began to speak.

"I never felt close to your parents." Her voice held a tremor. When he started to speak, she hurriedly continued. "They were always cordial to me, always. But I knew I wasn't what they hoped for in a daughter-in-law."

She held up a hand. "Please let me finish. Despite their…reservations… I could see that you were a close family, a loving one. I was happy for you."

As he watched her blink back tears, hot anger spurted. The anger not directed at her, but at those sorry excuses for parents who'd walked out on a child, leaving her to fend for herself.

"I overheard the conversation between you and your father in the library."

A sick feeling took up residence in the pit of Andrew's stomach. He recalled that conversation vividly, and his father hadn't minced words. "You heard what my father said? All of it?"

She nodded. "I heard what he said and what you said back to him."

Andrew frowned. He'd defended her. Stood up for her.

"You said he had to accept me, welcome me, or—" She swallowed hard as if there was something in her throat. "—or he was out of your life."

"That's right," Andrew said. "You were to be my wife. He needed to respect that decision, and you."

"I couldn't come between you." Tears, as plentiful as the raindrops on the window, slipped down her cheeks. "He's your father. You love him. He loves you."

Suddenly it all made sense. Okay, maybe not all, but a good portion. "You left because you didn't want to come between me and my father?"

"I know the importance of family. I also know the kind of bond that you and your father share isn't something to be tossed away lightly. It's something to be treasured." She lifted her drenched eyes. "Especially not over something that might not last."

"My father and I argue all the time. Those threats were common occurrences. But we didn't mean them." He was reaching for her, wanting to comfort and soothe, when her last comment registered. "You didn't believe we'd last?"

He saw indecision waver on her face and wondered if truth or lie would win the battle.

She lifted her chin. "No. We are so different."

"And everyone in your life that you've loved has left you."

Her sharp intake of breath told him the arrow had hit its target.

Andrew didn't mean to cause her pain, but he didn't need a psychiatry specialty to realize the abandonment she'd experienced as a child was at the root of all this. What he felt most guilty about was that he hadn't thought about that fact until this moment.

"I love you, Sylvie." He hadn't known he was going to say the words until they left his lips. "I never stopped loving you."

"I never stopped loving you, either." Her voice was so soft that for a second he feared he'd only imagined the words until he saw the emotion in her eyes. "But it doesn't change anything."

"We don't have to decide that tonight." He stood

and tugged her to her feet. "For now, just knowing that is enough."

He pulled her to him, wrapping his arms around her, simply holding her close. After a second, she relaxed, resting her head against his chest.

They stood there for the longest time, not speaking, drawing comfort from the closeness.

"Will you come to bed with me, Sylvie? Will you let me show you how much I love you?"

"Loving doesn't change—"

He covered her mouth with his, silencing the words. Perhaps realizing that she still loved him wouldn't change all that had happened between them. But she was back in his arms, and for the first time since she'd left, all was right in his world. That was enough for now.

The only threat to Andrew's happiness in the next twenty-four hours was a report from Seth that they'd discovered more blood clots in Mrs. Whitaker's legs. The treatment that had been ordered was appropriate, but Andrew hated being so far away.

He called Fern and spoke with her for a long time.

"What's the matter?" Sylvie asked, setting a bowl of popcorn on the coffee table.

Though he'd begun to pace, he abruptly dropped down on the sofa and blew out a harsh breath. "One of my patients back in Boston isn't doing well."

It was ridiculous, he told himself, to be so upset. Mrs. Whitaker was receiving the best medical treatment. She'd also lived almost nine decades on earth.

"She was my first patient when I started my concierge practice." He smiled, suddenly recalling how she'd told all her friends having such a wonderful—

and handsome—doctor was well worth the monthly fee. "She wielded a lot of influence in Boston. I owe a lot of my success to her."

Sylvie sat beside him on the sofa, their shoulders touching. "You care about her."

"Of course I do," Andrew asserted. "She's my patient."

"You care about her," Sylvie repeated.

He leaned his head back against the soft leather. "I do."

With gentle, soothing fingers, she pushed a lock of hair back from his face. "That's why you're such a good doctor. You really care."

Andrew said nothing, reveling in the sweet touch and the lilt of her voice.

"I think you need a distraction, something to make you forget your troubles for a few hours."

"We were going to watch a movie." Even as he said the words, Andrew knew the action flick they'd planned to watch was unlikely to hold his attention. Still, it was worth a try.

"I wasn't thinking of a movie."

Something about the sultry edge to her voice had him turning his head.

"Put your arm around me."

It was an easy order. He looped his arm around her shoulders. When she snuggled close, he felt some of the tension ease from his body.

"Did you ever make out with a girl on the sofa when you were growing up?"

"Sure," he said, intrigued by the direction the conversation had taken. "Make-out sessions is practically a teenage rite of passage."

"I never did."

"You're kidding me." Even as he spoke, his fingers began playing with her hair.

"I've told you my background." She gazed up at him through lowered lashes. "I was in foster homes. Most of them were fairly strict."

His lips curved slightly. "What made you think of youthful indiscretions?"

"You."

Andrew wasn't sure if it was the glass of wine he'd had with dinner or simple fatigue, but he was having difficulty following this conversation. "I don't understand."

"You're wearing jeans."

He glanced down. It was strange how he'd quickly grown so comfortable being casual. "What does that have to do with anything?"

"You look incredibly sexy in denim."

For a second he thought she was joking until he saw the heat in her eyes.

"You'll look incredibly sexy out of those jeans, too." She trailed a finger down his thigh.

Andrew inhaled sharply, and need for her surged, fast and strong.

He leaned in, his face so close that if she turned her head ever so slightly, their lips would meet. "You smell so good."

Her body quivered and she arched her neck back, giving him full access to the creamy skin of her neck. Her skin tasted as sweet as candy and he wanted to devour her.

"You missed some vital parts of your education living in foster homes," Andrew said before taking the lobe of her ear into his mouth and sucking gently.

She gasped. "I—I hardly think kissing someone on a sofa would be considered vital, much less educational."

Seeing no need to argue, Andrew stroked her back, smiling when he felt her begin to tremble—not with fear, he knew, but with need. Need for *him*. "I'm glad some randy teenage boy never kissed you on the sofa."

"Why?"

He captured her hand and brought her fingers to his lips, kissing each of them, spacing out each word with kisses. "Because you're mine."

"I wasn't yours back then," she pointed out.

For a second he reveled in the fact that she'd accepted that she was his, and he was hers.

Andrew trailed a finger down her cheek, his eyes on hers. "You were always mine. Even before we met, even before we got to know each other and fell in love, you were mine."

When she opened her mouth as if to protest, he closed it with a kiss that had her sighing. "And I am yours. Tell me that you're mine. I want to hear the words."

"You know how I feel about you," she murmured, trying to distract him by trailing kisses up his neck.

"Tell me, Sylvie." His voice held an intensity that even he didn't fully understand. "Tell me you're mine."

Her arms were woven around his neck, and before she rested her head against his chest, he saw her eyes close.

"I'm yours," she whispered. "For now."

He frowned, but before he could say anything more, she was kissing him with a heat that had fire coursing through his veins. Her hands were everywhere, tugging and pulling as she fought to rid him of his clothes.

It was a battle she was destined to win, but that didn't mean they had to race to the finish line. They had all night.

Lifting her hands from his belt buckle, Andrew cupped her head and closed his mouth over hers. The kiss started out sweet and gentle. Sylvie leaned forward and he felt the remaining tension leave her body. When he continued to kiss her as if they had all the time in the world, she wrapped her arms around his neck, sliding her fingers into his hair.

They kissed until he felt drugged with sensation. The only thing he knew was her. The only thing he wanted was her.

The kisses turned hotter, grew more intense until the fire in his blood burned as hot as the one in the hearth. He didn't just want his mouth on her—he had to touch.

The hands that had been traveling up and down her sides as they kissed moved upward, cupping her breasts through the thin cotton shirt. Through the fabric Andrew felt the hard tips as she pressed against his palms.

The next time his hands moved up, they slipped beneath her shirt, pushing aside the scrap of lace fabric. When his thumbs began to tease the tips, Sylvie moaned.

"Tell me what you want." His voice, low, husky and filled with need, sounded foreign to his own ears.

"We still have too many clothes on for what I want," she murmured.

He laughed, delighted with her honesty. "On that point we totally agree."

Giving her a hard, swift kiss, he began flinging off his clothes. "Race you."

She appeared to embrace the challenge. In a matter of seconds, her clothes lay on the floor in a heap beside his. Though he wanted to fill her, to be as close to her as was physically possible, he didn't rush.

Andrew nipped and kissed and took his time refamiliarizing himself with every inch of her body. When he finally did enter her, it was as if they were coming together for the first time.

Still, he didn't rush, but continued to make love to her until the pleasure broke over her with such force she cried out. Only then did he take his own release, following her over the edge while calling her name.

Spent and content, they lay there on the sofa, her body curled into his while his hand gently stroked her hair.

"It's like before," he murmured. "We can't seem to keep our hands off each other."

"Uncontrollable lust appears to be our cross to bear." She delivered the words with a straight face and made him laugh.

"I'll never get enough of you." The moment he said the words, he knew they were true. Now he just had to figure out how to make the second chance they'd been given work.

Chapter Sixteen

Sylvie considered attending the Wild 100 Artist Party at the National Museum of Wildlife Art a horrendous waste of money. The entry fee for the event was one hundred dollars. Certainly it would be fun to view the art and mingle with the artists before the sale, but the cost of attending was way out of her price range.

"Are you still upset I purchased the tickets without discussing it with you first?" Andrew took her elbow as they navigated the steps to the museum.

"What makes you think I'm upset?"

"You get quiet." His tone was easy and conversational. "That's what you do when you're upset. You barely spoke on the drive here."

She wasn't sure why she was making such a big deal out of nothing. Two hundred dollars was pocket change to an O'Shea. Maybe because it reminded her that, despite the past few days, they came from two different worlds. "You think you know me so well."

"I believe I'm getting to know you." He reached around her to open the door.

For a second Sylvie forgot all about the conversation as she inhaled the scent of him. She loved the way he smelled, of soap, shampoo and that subtle, expensive cologne. Tonight, even dressed casually, he looked as good as he smelled.

Though he'd considered wearing a suit, she'd convinced him that from everything she'd read, casual attire was de rigueur. He'd settled for jeans but had topped them with a sport coat and a cotton shirt. Her filmy dress with colors that brought to mind a Monet painting seemed to meet with his approval.

"If something is bothering you, you need to tell me." His tone was equitable, but some of the light that had filled his eyes when he heard his patient back in Boston was doing better had dimmed.

"I'm sorry." She shifted her gaze from the brochure she'd been handed. "It was kind of you to get the tickets. Thank you."

He took her arm and she leaned into him, brushing her lips across his cheek.

"Who are you?" A tiny smile hovered at the corners of his lips. "What have you done with my Sylvie?"

She rolled her eyes but shoved her sense of unease aside, determined to have a pleasant evening. "When I get stressed, I tend to get quiet. I don't know why. It probably has something to do with not wanting to let my emotions show."

Andrew grabbed a couple of glasses of champagne

from a passing waiter and handed one to Sylvie. "What's wrong with letting your emotions show?"

She shrugged and sauntered over to a painting of several red foxes. "This is very nice," she said to the artist, then moved on.

"You like red foxes," Andrew said. "You liked that other painting at the gallery. That was of a fox, too."

"I like the gallery one better." Sylvie lowered her voice so she wouldn't be overheard. The last thing she wanted was for the artist to think she was dissing her painting, which really was quite good. "That's just a personal preference thing. When I looked into the other one's eyes, it was almost as if I could read his thoughts."

She gave a little laugh. "Silly, I know."

"Not at all." His eyes softened. "Paintings speak to us."

His gaze settled on the one on permanent display, the wild-eyed buffalo he couldn't help noticing during the Sweet Adelines event. "It's like his gaze is following me wherever I go."

Sylvie glanced around. "Who?"

Andrew jerked his head in the direction of the bison. "Mr. Crazy."

Her gaze settled on the portrait and she laughed. "Yeah, definitely crazy eyes."

It was pleasant, Sylvie thought, strolling with Andrew through the gallery, chatting with artists. Several of those displaying paintings had stopped by her booth at the Taste of the Tetons and remembered her.

Warmth coursed through her veins like warm honey at the thought of being accepted as an artist in her own field in this vibrant community.

"I'm having fun tonight."

Andrew brushed a kiss against her hair. "You sound surprised."

"I used to believe I wasn't good at these kinds of events, but I'm starting to see that maybe I was mistaken." She let her gaze slide around the large room and realized with a shock that she recognized many in attendance. "I never thought I'd find a place where I belong, a place that felt so much like home."

The last of her words were drowned out by the rock classic blaring from Andrew's pocket.

He grimaced. "I forgot to silence it."

But when he pulled the phone from his pocket and his thumb moved to silence it, he paused instead, frowned, before bringing the phone to his ear. "Dr. O'Shea."

Not sure if this conversation was something she should overhear, Sylvie moved to the hors d'oeuvres table to study the selection. She wasn't particularly hungry, but it always paid to study the competition.

She'd just selected a grilled scallop wrapped in prosciutto when Andrew walked up. The light that had been in his eyes only moments earlier had vanished.

Without thinking, she held out the appetizer. "Want a bite?"

He shook his head.

Neither did Sylvie, not anymore. Since she'd taken it, other than tossing it into the trash, the only other option was to eat it. She popped it into her mouth, chewed and quickly swallowed.

"What's wrong?" she asked when they began to walk.

He still hadn't said a word. The muscle in his jaw worked.

"It's nothing."

"That kind of ridiculous answer never works with

you, and it doesn't with me, either. I know something isn't right."

The remark earned a nod.

"Fern, Mrs. Whitaker… She died." His voice wavered for a second, then steadied. "Seth called to tell me."

Seth Carstairs, his associate back in Boston.

Slipping her arm through his, Sylvie gave it a sympathetic squeeze. "I'm sorry. I know how much she meant to you."

"She was eighty-nine."

"Yes, and she was your first patient. She was special."

"I prefer not to discuss her right now."

Sylvie didn't press. She knew how hard it could be to have emotions near the surface that you needed to keep under control. But tonight, when they were home, she'd comfort him.

Because he'd taught her that was what you did when someone you loved was hurting.

"Tell me about Mrs. Whitaker." Sylvie waited until the valet had pulled the car around to ask.

"What do you want to know?" Andrew handed the young man a couple of bills and in less than a minute they were gliding down the highway.

It was a dark night, with only a sliver of a moon. The highway was surprisingly deserted and the headlight beams were the only light slicing the blackness.

Though Sylvie couldn't see Andrew's expression clearly, the tight set of his jaw and the way his fingers gripped the steering wheel told her emotion simmered just below the surface.

"What was special about her?" Sylvie cocked her

head. "It wasn't simply that she was your first patient when you opened your concierge practice."

That might have been part of it, but Sylvie didn't believe for a minute that was the whole of it.

"She lived down the street from my parents' home."

"You knew her when you were a little boy."

His fingers on the steering wheel relaxed. "Her children were older and they'd all moved away. Her backyard had this huge oak tree with a wooden playhouse. You had to climb a ladder and then part of the tree to get to it."

"Sounds dangerous and incredibly fun." Sylvie couldn't keep the smile from her voice.

"Tommy and I loved that tree."

Tommy. *Thomas.* The brother who'd died several years earlier. Sylvie tried to piece together the few things that Andrew had said about him. He'd been older and involved with the family business. He'd died in a car accident on the way to a Red Sox game. Never married and no children. It wasn't much, she realized.

"Did the Whitakers mind you were climbing their tree?"

He chuckled. "You'd think, because of liability and all that, but they didn't. In the summer, Mrs. Whitaker—her given name was Fern—would bring out a silver tray of cookies and lemonade for us. Climbing, she'd say, was hard work."

Impulsively Sylvie reached over and took his hand, lacing her fingers through his. She hoped the touch comforted him as much as it comforted her. "She sounds like a wonderful woman."

"She was." Affection filled his voice. "Tommy used to call her Granny Whitaker. I never had the guts."

"I think I'd have liked Thomas."

The hand she held tightened.

"You probably would have. Everyone did."

"What was he like?" She kept her tone easy, conversational as the darkness enveloped them in a warm cocoon.

"I'd say like my father, but knowing how you feel about him, that might give you the wrong impression." Andrew chuckled. "But it's true. Thomas was my father."

"I can't see your father climbing trees."

"People grow up." Andrew's tone gave nothing away. "Sometimes, often, they lose that adventurous spirit."

"Is that what happened to your brother?"

"Maybe. Probably," Andrew added after a moment. "He loved the company, had been groomed to be my father's successor. It was a perfect fit. Like my dad, he was a workaholic."

"At least he took time out for baseball."

Sylvie was unprepared for the oath that Andrew expelled and for the strained silence that followed.

Andrew turned off the highway toward Spring Gulch. It might have been wise to simply let the topic drop. Sylvie had never thought of herself as particularly wise.

"Does his death have something to do with baseball?" she asked. "I mean, I know he was on his way to a game when he died, but—"

"He was on his way to the game because I hounded him into going." Andrew's voice, low and guttural and filled with pain, tore at Sylvie's heartstrings. "I was concerned about all the hours he'd been working. I pushed and prodded until he agreed to meet me at Fenway. If I hadn't, he'd have been safe at the office, working."

"You don't know that. What happened to him was an accident. He could have been in an accident on the way home, or another day when he was going to the office." The hand he'd released now gripped his arm. "Inviting him to go to a game with you, hounding him to go to the game with you, doesn't make you responsible."

"Maybe not," he said after a long moment, "but I wish things had been different."

They'd reached the house that Sylvie had started to regard as "home" and pulled into the garage. A thought occurred to her as they stepped inside the house.

"Is taking the COO position some kind of penance?"

He didn't answer, just tossed his keys on the side table by the door and continued on into his bedroom. Several minutes later she heard the shower spray.

Sylvie stared down the hallway, unsure what to do. She didn't have any experience with families. She wasn't particularly good at interpersonal relationships. Her MO in the past had been to pull back or to run when things got sticky.

But she sensed that even if he didn't realize it, Andrew needed her tonight.

Returning to her own room, she got ready for bed. By the time she finished, the room next door was silent and dark.

Maybe he was asleep, she thought for a second, but knew in her heart that was only wishful thinking.

Hoping she wasn't going to make the situation worse, Sylvie reached for the doorknob and gave it a turn. It opened, which meant he hadn't locked her out.

She moved carefully through the room to the large king-size bed. Sylvie knew he preferred to sleep on the right side of the bed.

Pulling the sheet and light spread back, she crawled beneath the covers.

"Sylvie, I'm not in the mood—"

"Shhh." She snuggled close, wrapping her arms around his tense frame. "Go to sleep. Morning will be here all too soon."

After that night, Sylvie slept with him. Andrew had to admit that he liked falling asleep beside her and waking up with her every morning. He'd considered flying back to Boston for Mrs. Whitaker's funeral but then learned she'd been cremated and a memorial service was being planned closer to what had always been her favorite holiday, Thanksgiving.

The next week brought a change to their routine as Sylvie was busy preparing for Josie and Noah's wedding at the end of the week. He'd already been put on notice that she expected him to attend the pig-roast prenuptial dinner at the Campbells' home and the wedding on Saturday.

The one thing they hadn't discussed was that the end of the month was swiftly approaching, which meant his time to return to Boston was near.

Andrew knew it was cowardly, but he did his best to put that fact out of his mind. It was relatively easy to do, considering that the clinic remained short-staffed and he'd agreed to fill in while he was in town.

This meant he'd spend the early-morning hours with Sylvie and then head over to the clinic to see patients. Because they were both tired at the end of the day, they ate at home, sharing meals at the small table in the kitchen and then making love in the big bed.

Andrew had never been happier.

The night of the pig roast, he pulled on the blue jeans that no longer felt strange and the pair of cowboy boots Mitzi had surprised him with as a special thank-you for helping out at the clinic.

"I love your boots." Sylvie looked like a cowgirl herself in ankle-high boots, a light blue skirt and an oversize white shirt with a belt studded with multicolored stones cinched tight.

"You look nice." He moved to her and was pleased when she wrapped her arms around his neck and lifted her face for a kiss.

He tightened his arms around her, inhaling the scent of her that reminded him of cinnamon, sugar and everything delicious. Lowering his head, he nuzzled her neck. When he felt her breath quicken, he sensed victory. "No one is going to mind if we're a few minutes late."

"I'm bringing the cake, remember?"

Sensing he wasn't going to win this one, no matter how promising the path had appeared only moments earlier, Andrew reluctantly released her. "I'm still not sure why they wanted a cake tonight when they're going to have one at the wedding."

"A *traditional* one." Sylvie rolled her eyes. "Josie's father is very conservative, as are most of Noah's family. The cake I'm bringing tonight is just for them."

She'd shown him her masterpiece earlier, once she'd put on the finishing touches. It was what Sylvie called a "Lucky in Love" cake. Apparently Valentine's Day held special meaning to the couple, so the cake with its four layers tilted askew, containing hearts and stripes and checkerboard designs in black and white and red, was a tribute to their love.

"Are you ready to load it up?"

"I am."

They were driving Ethel to the party. Andrew had never arrived at any kind of social event in a van. But neither had he ever worn cowboy boots and jeans to a party.

They slid the cake box into the back of the vehicle. Because Josie's parents didn't live far, it would be a quick trip.

The talk remained on cakes on the drive over. "Our cook used to make us these wonderful birthday cakes. They weren't nearly as intricate and creative as the ones you do, but Carmen had a knack."

He smiled. "One year I asked for Teenage Mutant Ninja Turtles on my cake. She was horrified, but Donatello wielding a bo staff was on my cake."

"Sounds cute." Sylvie gave a chuckle.

"What was your favorite birthday cake?" Andrew wished he could withdraw the question the second it left his lips.

"I never had one," she said, her tone matter-of-fact. "Unless you count the ones I made myself."

"Did you go all out or keep them simple?"

"Some years simple. Other times I experimented." Her lips curved. "The only thing they had in common was they were always chocolate. I love chocolate cake."

He made a mental note, thinking that was something he should have already known. But then, they'd never celebrated her birthday together. Because hers wasn't until the fall...

"Your birthday is next week."

"A week from tomorrow, to be exact." She leaned back in the seat. "October 1."

The significance wasn't lost on him.

That was the day he planned to be back in Boston.

Chapter Seventeen

Sylvie lost track of Andrew halfway through the party. After dining on pork and an assortment of fancy salad, they'd dug into the cake. Then it was time to do some serious mingling.

While the term "pig roast" might have conjured up a more casual image, this prenuptial dinner was no more a backyard barbecue than Sylvie was a blue blood.

The large open area behind John and Dori Campbell's massive ranch home opened onto federal land and provided a stunning view of the mountains. The rich green of the perfectly manicured lawn was interrupted at strategic locations by bright patches of colors, the fall flowers adding their fragrance to the scent of pine.

As the nights were turning dark earlier, the backyard had been draped in hundreds—probably thousands—of lights strung from large poles wrapped in silver and gold ribbon, interspersed with flowers.

Linen tablecloths in a rich platinum shade covered the long tables where the guests dined off fine china with sterling silver utensils and sipped the finest wine out of crystal glasses.

Sylvie had expected the wedding party and their "plus ones" to be in attendance, as well as Josie and Noah's family. She hadn't expected half the population of Jackson Hole. Even the mayor, Tripp Randall, was there with his wife, as well as his parents, who were friends of John and Dori.

Kathy Randall cornered her when she was getting a "Crazy Coyote" margarita. "Have you thought any more about joining us?"

"I've thought about it." Sylvie took the frosty drink that reminded her of a morning sunrise and considered. She could continue as she had been, focusing primarily on her business. Or she could continue her recent forays into becoming part of the fabric of Jackson Hole. "I'd love to be part of your group."

"That's wonderful news." Kathy turned to the young man in the black pants and white shirt working the drink machine and smiled brightly. "I'll take one of those, too, please."

She slid a companionable arm around Sylvie's shoulders. "I'm so glad you moved here."

"That was nice of her to say," Andrew commented when Sylvie told him of her conversation with Kathy.

"She meant it, too." Sylvie expelled a satisfied sigh.

He was glad she was enjoying herself. They'd become separated after eating. Once Andrew had found her again, he'd taken her hand and guided her to the far end of the yard where a weathered fence separated the lawn from the wildlife area.

He knew this was her friend's party, but Josie was busy with her groom-to-be and Andrew wanted some alone time with her. Probably because of their earlier conversation, he felt unsure and apprehensive.

The knowledge that October 1 was next week had blown him away. He'd begun to feel as if he'd been in Jackson Hole forever, and having the real world intrude had been a rude awakening.

"Are you having fun?"

He hooked his boot on the bottom rail and slanted a glance in her direction. She sounded worried. She looked worried. He thought about teasing her but decided to be honest. "These are nice people."

"I saw you speaking with Tripp. He's Kathy Randall's son."

"He's an interesting guy. Did you know he used to manage a large health system back East before he moved back to Jackson Hole?"

"I didn't know that."

"He's very progressive when it comes to the health needs of those who live in Jackson Hole." Andrew turned to face Sylvie. "Talking to Tripp made me realize how isolated I'd become from the medical community in Boston."

"Well, that won't be a problem for much longer." Though her tone was light, something in her eyes warned of an approaching storm.

He inclined his head. "What do you mean?"

"When you return you won't be practicing medicine anymore, will you?"

He reached out for her, intending to what? Reassure her that he wouldn't be leaving? As much as he wished that didn't have to happen, he knew he'd be returning to Boston. But if he had his way, she'd be coming with him.

It was odd how it had all worked out. He'd come to Wyoming in order to get to know her better so that he could purge her from his system. Instead he was more deeply in love with her than ever.

The thought of spending the rest of his life without her was intolerable. He'd convince her to come with— there was no alternative.

Now, however, wasn't the time to push that request. Tonight they would enjoy the evening. Then they would go back to Boston, together.

Sylvie put the thought of Andrew's upcoming departure from her mind. Or tried.

It was Josie's wedding day. The twenty-fourth of September had dawned sunny and without a cloud in the sky.

Happy the bride the sun shines on.

She smiled as she watched Poppy, Josie's sister-in-law and matron of honor, adjust the bride's veil.

There had been a time when Sylvie imagined herself walking down the aisle to Andrew. She'd planned on making a life with him in Boston.

Though she'd been wrong to run off in the way she had, she believed that if she hadn't, she'd have withered and died away. In her heart she'd known what she wanted but hadn't been willing to demand it.

She hadn't let Andrew see her, not really. She hadn't

had the courage to share her true self with him. For some reason, that had been easier to do here in Wyoming.

Maybe because she'd begun to change in the three months she'd been here. Or maybe because she felt a part of the world here, in a way that would never have been possible in Boston. The acceptance she'd found here had allowed her to grow.

In Boston she could have been married to Andrew for twenty years and still be an outsider. Pursuing a business would have been difficult given the social expectations for a member of the O'Shea family.

The heavy sigh was as out of place in the happy dressing area as a stick of margarine would be in her kitchen. Relieved that no one appeared to have noticed, Sylvie glanced into the mirror in front of her and fussed with her hair.

Cassidy had come in earlier to work her magic on the bride and her attendants. Sylvie's normally sleek do was now a riot of curls topped by a thin band of flowers. Her cocktail-length dress, a rich periwinkle blue, made her eyes look like violets.

When Cassidy had pulled out the huge cosmetics bag, Sylvie was worried. Normally her use of makeup was a few swipes of mascara and some lip gloss. But she had to admit, the gray shadow on her lids brought out not only the color in her eyes but made them look larger, more mysterious.

Sylvie smiled into the mirror at the ridiculous thought. The base made her skin look creamy with a hint of dew, and the lipstick—Passionate—added depth to her mouth.

She looked…pretty.

"I'm so happy we could share this day together."

Sylvie turned, only then realizing that Josie had crossed the room to her. "You look amazing," she said to her friend. "Like a princess."

The sleeveless ball-gown-style dress with the intricate beading suited Josie's figure. She was a beautiful woman, but the unmitigated joy in her eyes made her glow.

"I can't wait to walk down that aisle and marry Noah." Josie's voice softened the way it always did when she spoke of her future husband. She reached out and grasped Sylvie's hand. "Thanks for agreeing to be part of my special day."

"I was surprised you asked me." Sylvie had never quite had the nerve to ask Josie exactly why she'd asked her. "Especially only months from your wedding, when you already had enough bridesmaids."

"I felt a connection with you from the beginning." Josie squeezed the hand she still held. "It was as if we were sisters separated from birth. Are you sure your father's name isn't John Campbell?"

Sylvie laughed. "I'm honored."

"When you plan your wedding, I—"

"That's a long time in the future." Sylvie kept her tone light. "If ever."

"I thought you and Andrew…"

"I suppose anything is possible," Sylvie said and was relieved to see the worry leave her friend's eyes. "But this is your special day. We can discuss my special day another time. Deal?"

"Deal." Josie gave her hand a shake. "I think it's time we do this."

"It's definitely time for you to walk down that aisle."

Sylvie nodded for emphasis, her tone equally light-hearted.

In less than an hour, Josie Campbell and Noah Anson joined their lives together.

There was only one bad moment. That was when Josie looked into Noah's eyes when they said their vows. A promise made to stick tight through the good times and the bad, to build a life together.

Sylvie wasn't a crier. She didn't shed tears over sentimental cards or the commercials aired at holiday times. But seeing the promise in Josie's and Noah's eyes and knowing they meant every word brought tears to her eyes.

She blinked them back before anyone could notice or she embarrassed herself by letting them fall. They hit again when she was walking down the aisle at the end of the ceremony and her gaze locked with Andrew's.

The sight of him with that smile meant for only her had Sylvie's heart turning into a sweet, heavy mass in her chest. Was it her curse in life to want what she couldn't have?

A father. A mother. A home and a family. And now the man she loved.

For a second, as she returned to the front of the church to pose for pictures, she found herself wondering if it would have been better if Andrew had never come to Jackson Hole. Perhaps agreeing to spend the past few weeks with him had been a mistake, too.

He'd come to get her out of his system and she'd agreed to spend time with him. She'd owed him. Now that debt had been paid.

But she'd paid a high price, because now she knew

what she hadn't known then. Without him her heart would never be whole again.

The reception at the Spring Gulch Country Club lasted until 1:00 a.m. There was a sit-down dinner featuring steak and lobster followed by dancing to a live band.

From the number of flowers, it appeared the family had bought out every florist shop in the state of Wyoming. Andrew sat beside her at the head table.

By the time he'd reached the age of thirty, Andrew had been in his share of weddings. He had to admit this had been one of the most enjoyable. Sylvie was in high spirits and had even allowed him to escort her out on the dance floor.

What she lacked in basic skills, she made up in natural rhythm. The truth was, he didn't care if she could dance a single step. He simply wanted her in his arms.

"You smell terrific." It was a different scent, light and floral with a hint of sultry.

"French perfume," Sylvie confided. "My bridesmaid's gift from Josie."

"It's sexy as hell." He twirled her around, then dipped her low. "But your other fragrance is still my favorite."

Laughing and breathless, she clung to him as they straightened and then began to move to the lilting melody. "I don't usually wear perfume."

"You do." He leaned close, brushing his lips across her ear. "It smells a little like cinnamon and vanilla with a touch of a yeasty earthiness."

She tilted back her head and gazed into his eyes. "Are you saying I smell like a bakery?"

God, she's lovely.

"If the apron fits, wear it."

She laughed again. "That is so lame."

"I'm having difficulty concentrating." He lowered his voice so his next words were for her ears only. "I keep wondering what you're wearing under that dress."

"Why don't we go home and you can find out?"

Andrew's body reacted to the words. He could see her lying stretched out on the bed wearing only those high heels and silk stockings.

He was ready to walk out the door, but as he glanced around the room, his enthusiasm was tempered by reality. It wasn't even midnight and the reception was in full swing. Still, he was ready to carry this party on home. Not that he wasn't having fun. The dinner, the champagne and Sylvie's amazing cake had made for an enjoyable evening so far.

Being seated at the head table had given him a chance to get acquainted with Benedict's brothers— also physicians—as well as spend time with his beautiful date, who sparkled tonight like the brightest gem in a showcase.

Yet it had been a long day. The knowledge that they didn't have to get up at three to bake—someone named Lexi Delacourt was filling in—meant he and Sylvie could enjoy themselves for as long as they wanted once they got home.

"How long do you have to stay?" He kept his tone nonchalant. She was a bridesmaid. This was her friend's reception. If Sylvie felt she needed to close down the party, she'd hear no complaints from him.

"I don't believe it matters," she said. "We'll just

need to say our goodbyes and then we should be able to slip away."

Saying their goodbyes took a little longer than Andrew had hoped, but within forty-five minutes they were home.

The first thing Sylvie did when she walked through the door was to plop down on the sofa and slip off those sexy stilettos.

Andrew felt a pang when he saw them drop to the floor.

"It was a beautiful wedding, but I'm glad it's done." She raked a hand through her curls, dislodging several flowers from the ring.

"Before you get too comfortable." He held out his hand, and when she took it, he pulled her up against him. "Let's dance."

He began to sway.

"We don't have any music," she said even as her steps followed his.

He brushed his lips across her hair. "We make our own music."

She gave a happy sigh and settled against him, her body molding to his, soft where he was hard.

Rock hard.

"If you wanted to dance," she said into his shirtfront, "we could have stayed at the reception."

"If we'd been on the dance floor, I couldn't have done this." He tipped her face up to his, then lowered his mouth over hers.

She tasted like wine and cake, an erotic combination that fueled the fire coursing through his veins.

He wanted this woman. He loved this woman. And he would find a way that she would be his.

Not just for tonight, but forever.

Chapter Eighteen

Andrew rolled out of bed the next morning at nine o'clock. He decided he'd never again take for granted sleeping past 3:00 a.m. It had been nearly that time when he and Sylvie finally fell into an exhausted slumber.

Instead of heading straight for the shower, he glanced down at the bed. Sylvie lay sprawled on her back, one arm crooked over her eyes as if shielding them from light. The pretty curls disheveled from last night's love-making only made her more beautiful.

He wanted to wake her, to make love to her again and feel that connection, the bond they'd forged. Andrew knew the difference between making love and having sex. Last night had been all about love.

He'd come here to get her out of his heart. Instead his love for her had only grown deeper. He knew she loved Jackson Hole, but if she gave Boston a chance he knew she could love it there, too.

She could start a bakery there. His family had connections, lots of them, and could steer business her way until she got a good foothold. He understood her passion for creating now and would encourage those efforts.

If she liked his condo, they could live there. If it didn't suit her, they would shop around until she found a place that felt like home to her.

Andrew thought of his conversation with Gabe and Joel about building a home in Spring Gulch. That had just been a pipe dream. His life was in Boston. His future was with O'Shea Sports.

It wasn't the life he'd have chosen, but running the company would be his tribute to Thomas.

Sylvie stirred and for a second he thought she was waking up, but she merely rolled over and snuggled into the pillow. Giving up medicine would be difficult, but at least he would have Sylvie to ease the transition.

They would have a good life. He tried to imagine her back in Boston, but the image remained fuzzy.

After his shower, he dressed, then made coffee. He'd wait to make breakfast until Sylvie was awake. He was scrolling through his email when his phone rang. His father's picture flashed on the screen.

"Dad. How are you?"

"Very good." Despite the almost twenty-five hundred miles that separated them, the excitement in his father's voice came through loud and clear. "Excellent, in fact."

Andrew found himself smiling into the phone. "What's

going on? Did that new technology the engineers were working on pan out?"

It was an educated guess. Though his dad loved his family, nothing got him more revved up than business successes. And Andrew was aware that the R & D department had been working on several ways to refine the engineering and performance of their bestselling running shoe.

"That project is coming along nicely," his father said, almost as if they were talking about a minor change of little consequence. "This is bigger. That's why I need you back. I've sent the Gulfstream."

Andrew took a drink of the Ethiopian blend he'd just brewed. Obviously his brain wasn't yet firing on all circuits. "You sent the Gulfstream where?"

His dad was very particular about the use of the corporate jet. If he'd sent it out, the news had to be big.

"To Jackson Hole. Weren't you listening to me?" His father's voice lashed like a whip.

Andrew resisted the urge to chuckle. His father must be revved up to use what Corinne called his "head honcho" tone with a family member.

"I heard you say something big is happening."

"Not big—huge." The excited tremor returned to his father's voice. "We're about to finalize the acquisition of a European mobile fitness start-up."

"Wasn't that the deal Corinne had been working on?" Andrew vaguely recalled his sister mentioning something about a company with a GPS fitness tracking app. If it was that particular deal, it was worth about two hundred and forty million dollars.

"Your sister made the initial contacts, was involved

in the preliminary negotiations, but I want you here to close the deal."

Andrew wondered what his sister thought about being tossed out during the sprint to the finish, but he shoved the thought aside. He'd attempted to advocate on Corinne's behalf, but his father could not be swayed. O'Shea men had run the company for the hundred years since it was founded, and that was the way it would continue.

If only he hadn't hounded Thomas into coming to that game with him, it would be his brother closing the deal. Thomas would have been as excited as his father and Corinne over all the possibilities. Andrew would have to dig deep to find even a modicum of enthusiasm for the project.

After confirming he would indeed fly back to Boston that afternoon, Andrew clicked off and laid the phone on the table.

He hoped Sylvie would be able to make the trip with him today, but he would understand if she had to stay behind for a few days to close up her business here.

"You're leaving?"

Sylvie stood in the doorway, wearing nothing but the white shirt he'd had on last night. It hung halfway to her bare thighs. Her expression gave nothing away.

"My dad called." He gestured to the coffeemaker, gripped with a sudden feeling of unease. "I made a pot. Ethiopian blend. Your favorite."

Without even sparing the countertop where the coffeepot rested a single glance, she crossed the room, stopping a couple of feet from him. "What did your father want?"

"He wants me to come home." Andrew might have been speaking with a statue. She didn't even blink.

"I thought you had until October 1 to give him your decision."

He frowned, puzzled. "What decision?"

"About whether you'd be returning to Boston or not."

"My returning to Boston has never been in question."

She flinched as if she'd been slapped. "I see."

"What do you see?" The question spurted out with more edge than he'd intended.

"I see," she said slowly and deliberately, "that you came back here to get me out of your system. You've accomplished your mission. Now you're leaving."

The light that had shone so brightly in her eyes last night had vanished.

"You don't understand." He stepped forward, grasped her hands. Relief surged when she didn't pull away. "I want you to come with me."

The flicker in her eyes was all the encouragement Andrew needed. The words tumbled out. "If you don't like my condo in the Millennium Towers, we can do some house-hunting while we're there. You can even scout locations for your bakery. It will be good, Sylvie. You and I can build a life together there."

She tugged her hands free, took a step back. "I have a life here, in Jackson Hole."

His heart plummeted, but somehow, when he spoke his voice was calm. "Of course you do. And we can come back every winter and see your friends. They can come and see us in Boston as often as you want."

"You're planning on working for your father."

"I won't be working for him in the traditional sense

of the word." His tone had stiffened, despite his best efforts to control it. "He'll be the CEO of O'Shea Sports. I'll be COO. We'll each have duties and responsibilities."

"You'll be working all the time."

Though Andrew wanted to reassure her, he wouldn't lie. "Initially, possibly."

"Probably," he qualified at her probing look. "But once I get up to speed, it won't be as much."

"Will you be able to practice medicine?"

"No." He'd done his best not to think of what he'd be giving up, and he found himself resenting her for bringing it up. "There won't be time."

Sadness swept across her face. "There won't be time for me, either."

"It'll be hectic at first, but—"

She raised a hand. "The position will consume your life, like it does for your father, like it did for your brother."

The mention of Thomas had him going cold. "What are you saying, Sylvie? Spit it out."

"I'm not going with you."

"You can come later. I realize you have obligations here. I was hoping you could fly back with me today, but I understand—"

"No." She met his gaze. "I'm not going back to Boston with you, Andrew. I can't watch you lose yourself, give up your passion for medicine as a way of atoning for your brother's death."

He'd stepped forward but stopped a foot from her. She might look small and vulnerable in his shirt, but her eyes, as well as her tongue, were razor sharp.

"I care about you too much." She closed her eyes,

and for the first time, he noticed the tears shimmering on the edges of her lashes.

"If you cared about me, you'd come with me." It was as close to begging as he'd ever come with anyone. "Please, Sylvie, come with me. Make a life with me in Boston."

"You giving up your dream for someone else's would only tear us apart."

"You're still running scared, aren't you?" His humorless laugh sounded harsh even to his own ears. "You can't, you won't, make a commitment because you're scared it won't work."

"That's not it," she protested. "It's—"

"You're a coward."

Her spine stiffened even as her eyes turned dark as midnight. "You won't stand up to your father. You won't make him understand how important medicine is to you. You won't fight for your sister when you know it's the right thing to do. Who's the coward, Andrew?"

"You think you know me so well. You think you know what I want?" He ground out the words. "You don't know anything."

Without another word, he brushed past her and headed down the hall. Pulling his suitcase from the closet, he dumped the contents from the drawers into it and snapped it shut.

"What are you doing?"

It was a silly question.

"I have a plane to catch. I'll have someone come in and clean up the house, so don't worry about it."

"Andrew."

The soft sound of his name on her lips had him turning, had hope rising inside him.

"Don't go."

The hope deflated like an untied balloon. "I have obligations."

She gave a brisk nod.

"There's a birthday present for you in the extra bedroom." He caught the scent of French perfume when he strode past her.

Riding on temper, he didn't slow his pace until he was behind the wheel of the car. As he pulled out of the driveway, it struck him that this time he was the one leaving, not her.

The rest of the day, the day they were supposed to spend together, Sylvie held out hope that Andrew would come back. She kept busy cleaning the house but resisted the impulse to pack up her things until the light in the sky dissolved into darkness.

She packed her belongings and was already in Ethel and ready to pull out of the driveway when she remembered Andrew's parting words. He'd left a present for her in the extra bedroom, the one they'd kept closed off.

For a second, Sylvie thought about leaving the gift behind, but that was only angry thinking. Reluctantly she went back inside the house that held so many good memories.

The present was large and covered in brown paper. She looked at it for a long moment, then carefully unwrapped it.

The painting of the fox, the one standing on the boulder looking over his shoulder, stared back at her.

Aren't you coming after me?

Sylvie closed her eyes. Her heart swelled, pressing against her lungs, causing her breath to come short and shallow. Tears filled her eyes until the image of the red fox blurred.

Aren't you coming after me?

It was the same way Andrew had looked at her, with such hope and longing. The way he'd looked at her before those soft gray eyes had turned to steel.

"No," she whispered, though there was no one in the house to hear. "I won't. I can't come with you."

As the trickle of tears became a stream, Sylvie cried for what could have been and what now would never be.

Chapter Nineteen

Sylvie had offered to take Lexi out to lunch on Monday as a thank-you for filling in for her on Saturday night. Though she didn't know the woman well, Lexi had a busy family life and it couldn't have been much fun for her getting up in the middle of the night to bake.

As she wasn't feeling particularly sociable, Sylvie found herself hoping that Lexi would be too busy to meet. Instead she had enthusiastically agreed. They'd set a time and place. Noon at Perfect Pizza.

Sylvie arrived a few minutes early and found Lexi already waiting. The woman was pretty with dark hair cut in a stylish bob. Her wrap pencil skirt in gray and a thin black sweater made Sylvie feel underdressed in her blue cardi and printed skirt.

It had been hard to care about her appearance the

past couple of days. It had been hard to care about anything at all.

"Sylvie." Lexi's voice rang with welcome. "I'm so glad you suggested we meet for lunch. I've been wanting to get better acquainted."

When Lexi took her hands and pulled her close for a brief hug, Sylvie had to blink back unexpected tears.

"I owe you so much for helping me out Saturday night." Sylvie returned the hug. "It would have been so hard to get up that day. I don't think any of my customers would have gotten my best work."

"Are you ready to order?" the person behind the wooden counter asked, putting an end to the conversation.

They decided to split a small pizza with ham and pineapple with cream cheese and were given two large amber-colored plastic glasses for iced tea.

The fact that this was the same type of pizza she and Andrew had shared brought a heaviness to her chest. It took all the strength Sylvie had to fill her glass and grab some silverware from the beverage station.

She followed Lexi to the window, slid into the booth made out of knotty pine opposite her luncheon companion and forced what she hoped was a cheery smile.

The last thing Sylvie wanted to do was talk about herself, so she kept the conversation focused on Lexi. She learned that, like Poppy, Lexi was a social worker.

"After our last baby was born, I decided to be a stay-at-home mom and do some catering every now and then."

"Do you miss the social work?"

"Sometimes, but not enough to try to make it gel with the crazy schedules of my husband and kids."

Lexi took a sip of iced tea and her gaze grew thoughtful. "In a relationship, there has to be compromise."

"You also have to be true to who you are."

If Lexi was startled by the vehemence in Sylvie's tone, it didn't show. "Absolutely. We all have to decide how much we're willing to compromise, how far we can go and still be true to ourselves. I faced that when Nick and I first met."

Sylvie knew Lexi's husband was a popular family-law attorney in Jackson Hole. That was about all she knew. She gave Lexi an encouraging smile.

"I met Nick when he was injured in a skiing accident. He'd lost his memory."

"Are you kidding?"

Lexi smiled and lifted her fingers in some sort of scouting salute. "Bizarre, but true."

"He didn't know who he was? Not at all?"

"Not for quite a while."

Sylvie pushed her plate aside and leaned forward, resting her elbows on the table, glad she'd decided on this lunch. There was nothing like a case of amnesia to take your mind off your own troubles. "What happened?"

"I helped get him settled while we searched for his identity. In the process, we fell in love and began to plan a life together."

"That's very romantic."

"When his memory began to return, we discovered that he lived in Dallas, that he and his father had a law practice there."

"He gave it up to stay here with you." Sylvie sighed. It was the kind of happy ending she wished she and Andrew had been able to achieve.

"It wasn't that simple." Lexi's eyes grew distant with the memory. "It was a large, thriving law practice and his father depended on Nick. He asked me to move there with him."

"You said no."

"Initially," Lexi admitted. "My life was here, my job, my friends. I had a daughter. Addie was seven at the time. I couldn't just uproot her."

"What happened?"

"We compromised. We would spend part of the year in Texas and part of the year here. It couldn't be fifty-fifty because of Addie's schooling." Lexi stared at the last piece of pizza and picked it up. "Oh, what the heck?"

"That couldn't have been easy."

Lexi paused, the pizza near her lips. "Few things in life seldom are. It was a difficult couple of years, but Nick and I were together and that was the important thing, to Addie and to me. During the following years, his father added several more attorneys to the practice. This allowed Nick to spend more time building his practice in Jackson Hole. Now he only consults with his father on special cases."

Sylvie thought of Andrew. Thought about compromise. Thought about how far she was willing to go.

For the first time in forty-eight hours, the tightness in her chest eased. She met the other woman's gaze. "Lexi, I need your help."

If Sylvie could have left that day for Boston, she'd have done it. But she had clients and obligations and Lexi couldn't fill in for her until after the first.

She purchased a plane ticket with the last of her savings and hoped that Andrew would welcome her. She loved him, and between them, surely they could find a way to compromise.

The painting of the fox hung in her small living quarters. Each time she looked at it, she assured the fox that, yes, she was going after Andrew.

There was a chill in the air the morning of her birthday. She baked for her clients and went about making her deliveries. Other than Josie, who was still on her honeymoon, no one else knew that today was her birthday. Sylvie didn't mention it.

If she did, they might want her to go out and celebrate. She had to pack and get her sleep. Tomorrow she had an early flight to catch.

Her phone rang just as she was finishing up the last of her deliveries. "This is Sylvie."

"Hey, Sylvie, Keenan McGregor. I need a favor."

Sylvie tried to keep the surprise from her voice. "Sure. Anything."

"Great."

Was that relief she heard?

"Mitzi is convinced she lost her earring when we stopped over to your house."

For a second Sylvie was confused. As far as she could recall, Mitzi had never stopped into the Mad Batter. Then she realized he was speaking of the house in Spring Gulch, down the street from his. The one where she'd lived with Andrew.

"I cleaned the house before I closed it up," Sylvie told him. "I didn't find any earring. Are you sure she didn't lose it somewhere else?"

"She's certain she was wearing it there. Would you

mind stopping over there this afternoon and checking inside?"

"I locked the door and left the key inside."

"There's a keypad on the garage door. Surely you
remember the code?"

"Yes, but I—"

"It would mean a lot to me, uh, to us, if you'd look."

Sylvie wasn't quite sure how she felt about going
back inside. There were so many memories, including
the argument with Andrew. She'd done everything she
could to stay positive this week, but going back inside
could derail her optimistic mood. Still, Keenan and
Mitzi had been kind to her.

"What does it look like?"

For a moment there was only silence. "What does
what look like?"

"The earring Mitzi lost."

"Uh, like an earring."

Men, she thought with an exasperated smile. "I
mean, is it a hoop or a stud or—"

"Silver hoop," he said quickly. "With some scrollwork on the hoop."

"I would have thought I'd have seen it…"

"But you will go over and check."

"I will." She paused. "Can you meet me there? We
can both look."

She thought she heard him mutter something about
three being a crowd but knew she must have misheard.

"I'm tied up at the airport. Just call me if you find
it."

"Okay." Then, because he sounded so stressed, she
added, "I'll head over there right now."

When they ended the conversation, she stared at the

phone in her hand for a long moment. Likely it would be a wasted trip, but it would pass the time.

And she would be helping a friend. Wasn't that what life was all about in Jackson Hole?

Sylvie drew the van to a stop in front of the house. The lights were on inside, and a car she didn't recognize sat in the driveway. Whoever was inside wasn't trying to be sneaky, which ruled out a burglar. That left only two possibilities.

Andrew's friend had returned to Jackson Hole. Or he was letting another friend use the home.

If Keenan hadn't sounded so desperate, Sylvie wouldn't have gotten out of her van. But she'd promised. Perhaps whoever was living in the home now had found the earring. Not likely, but possible.

She glanced down at her jeans and sweater, wishing she'd dressed up a bit more. But it was too late now. She'd driven all the way out here and she was going to see it through.

When no one came to the door after she knocked, Sylvie rang the bell. The music playing inside abruptly stopped and she heard someone moving inside.

Straightening her shoulders, she pasted a smile on her face.

The smile froze when Andrew opened the door.

Maybe she was hallucinating. Maybe it wasn't him standing there in gray pants and a white shirt rolled up to the elbows. Maybe it wasn't him staring at her with solemn gray eyes.

"Hello, Sylvie." He stepped back, pushing the door farther open. "Won't you come in?"

No mirage.

She fought to find her voice. "I—I... Keenan said Mitzi lost something here. An earring, a silver hoop with some scrollwork. I told him I cleaned before I left the house, but he was so adamant I stop over and check—"

She was babbling. Without him saying a word, she suddenly understood there was no lost earring.

"Mitzi didn't lose an earring, did she?"

"No. No lost earring." He smiled. "I wanted to see you."

"You're here." Her gaze searched his face. "What are you doing here?"

"I can't be anywhere else but where you are. I've missed you, Sylvie."

Tears stung the backs of her eyes, but she blinked them back. "What about your job?"

"You were right. My career is medicine. My sister is the new COO of O'Shea Sports."

"I thought your dad didn't want a female."

"He's come to realize she's the best O'Shea for the job."

Something in those watchful gray eyes told her he'd had more than a little to do with his father's change of heart.

"I have a plane ticket to Boston tomorrow." She blurted out the words.

A look of puzzlement blanketed his face. "Why?"

"I thought you were there and I realized that I can't be anywhere else but where you are."

"Well, I'm here and I'm not going anywhere."

Suddenly she was in his arms.

He held her tightly.

"I love you, Sylvie." He let go of her long enough

to reach into his pocket. "This must have been in my drawer, because I found it when I got to Boston and unpacked."

The emerald-cut diamond caught the overhead light, sending colors sparkling in the air.

"It was yours," she said.

"No." He slipped it on her finger, his gaze never leaving hers. "It's yours. It's always been yours. If you want it."

She nodded, unable to push words past the massive lump in her throat. But she didn't need to speak for a long time, because his mouth covered hers and suddenly he was kissing her and she was kissing him back.

Kisses that spoke of promises made and promises that would be kept, of love lost and love found.

"Come with me." He stepped back and took her hand. "We have some celebrating to do."

"I thought that's what we were doing."

He grinned, and her world, which had been off balance since he'd walked out the door last week, righted itself.

She laced her fingers with his. After only a few steps, she stopped and sniffed the air. "I smell cake. Chocolate cake."

"Well, it is your birthday…"

Pleasure rippled through her. "You bought me a cake. No one ever bought me a cake."

"I *baked* you a cake."

The creation sat on the small table in the kitchen. He'd topped the double-layer chocolate with a slew of flickering candles that doubtless added up to twenty-seven.

It was the most beautiful cake she'd ever seen. She clasped her hands together. "It's lovely."

"Part of it fell." He grimaced. "I had to add more frosting to make the top even."

Her heart swelled. "It's perfect."

"You know what's perfect?"

"The cake," she said firmly.

"You're perfect." He wrapped his arms around her. "For me."

"Hey, that's what I was going to say."

Andrew chuckled. "Happy birthday, my love."

As his lips closed over hers, Sylvie held him tight, knowing they were both right where they belonged.

That was the greatest gift of all.

* * * * *

Don't miss out on previous books in Cindy Kirk's
RX FOR LOVE *series,*
THE DOCTOR'S VALENTINE DARE,
THE M.D.'S UNEXPECTED FAMILY
and
READY, SET, I DO!
Available now wherever Mills & Boon Cherish
books and ebooks are sold.

MILLS & BOON®

Cherish™

EXPERIENCE THE ULTIMATE RUSH OF FALLING IN LOVE

A sneak peek at next month's titles...

In stores from 11th August 2016:

- **Stepping Into The Prince's World** – Marion Lennox
  and **A Maverick and a Half** – Marie Ferrarella
- **Unveiling The Bridesmaid** – Jessica Gilmore *and*
  A Camden's Baby Secret – Victoria Pade

In stores from 25th August 2016:

- **The CEO's Surprise Family** – Teresa Carpenter *and*
  A Word with the Bachelor – Teresa Southwick
- **The Billionaire From Her Past** – Leah Ashton *and*
  Meet Me at the Chapel – Joanna Sims

Available at WHSmith, Tesco, Asda, Eason, Amazon and Apple

Just can't wait?
Buy our books online a month before they hit the shops!
visit www.millsandboon.co.uk

These books are also available in eBook format!

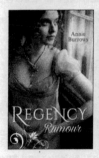
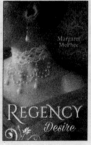